HERSELF IN LOVE

Marianne Wiggins

HERSELF IN LOVE

and other stories

Viking

VIKING
Viking Penguin Inc.
40 West 23rd Street,
New York, New York 10010, U.S.A.

First American Edition
Published in 1987

"Stonewall Jackson's Wife" first appeared in *The Yale Review*;
"Insomnia" in *Woman's Journal*; "3 Geniuses," under the title
"On the Nature of Sound and Color in the Universe," in *Formations*;
and "Herself in Love" in *Granta 17*.

ISBN 0-670-81552-7
Library of Congress Catalog Card Number 86-40499
(CIP data available)

Printed in the United States of America
Set in Baskerville

For Mac, without whom I

CONTENTS

Ridin' up in Front with Carl and Marl

'Climb on in,' Marl says to Dolores. 'You look pooped.'

She throws her weight, which is considerable, across the front seat of the Dodge and pushes the car door open on the passenger side, and the shift in weight causes the elastic strap of her brassiere to bind above her diaphragm, so she says, 'Come on, Dolores,' almost breathlessly. She straightens up and adds, 'I ain't goin' to see you traipsin' through this county all alone this time of night.'

Dolores waits a second. She looks like she's guessing at a question on a game show, then she says, 'I'm not in the mood for company, Marlene, the truth be told.'

'Is that a fac',' Marl states. 'Well, I'm not in the mood much neither, especially for yours. But my horryscope this mornin' said, "Plan to pick up skinny ol' Dolores on the road this evenin'," so don't run foul of good advice,

3

girl. I'm a Cancer – that's the crab, you know. You gettin' in?'

Marl looks at Dolores and Dolores looks at Marl. It wouldn't surprise Marl none if Dolores halfway disappeared just then, if she de-materialized into the atmosphere the way they do on 'Star Trek'. Every time Marl sees that trick on 'Star Trek', she thinks that it's the same old trick the Cheshire cat did back in 'Alice Through the Looking Glass', so that's nothin' new. She's seen things disappear and sort of fade-in fade-out in the middle of her hot spells, so she wouldn't be surprised if one day she was lookin' at Dolores swingin' in the yard on that ol' dinky swing left over by the other tenants and a part of her just disappeared, her ol' skinny neck and shoulders, for instance, or her skinny ol' thoracic region. There's this European painter that paints people with big holes in them, holes as big as windows where you see the clear blue sky and white clouds through their thoracic regions, though Marl couldn't begin to try to tell you this ol' painter's name. Names seem to go along with hot spells in that they come and go at random, mostly go. It wouldn't surprise Marl none if one day she was lookin' at Dolores and Dolores started to evaporate. For one thing, she's a skinny girl – looks about thirteen and she never did fill out. For another thing, she's pale and cloudy as ammonia – moody, too; always sittin' on that dinky swing in a pair of Joe Dean's cut-offs and those runnin' shoes she claims she got at discount out at K-Mart. The girl is strange – not strange in any way that you could say, 'Oh, you know, all she eats is seeds and berries,' or, 'You know, she claims she can make her palms bleed . . .' She's strange the way a day can seem real strange because of real low pressure – strange the way an old unoccupied house can feel real strange, like these old houses down here on the James and Appomattox. Never meant for forced oil heat, they seem pre-occupied, same as Dolores. Ghostlike, some cold wood-smellin' mist inhabits them, and though Marl would never go so far as to testify Dolores is possessed, she does worry 'bout the girl the same way everybody used to worry 'bout ol'Ginny Tibbetts when Ginny took to blowin' up those cat's-eye marbles in her oven to see what kind of pretty 'stained glass sculptures' she could make. Of course the mess Ginny made inside that oven was none of Marl's business just like Dolores's 'hobbies' aren't any of her business, either, still Marl can't help herself from proffering advice. Carl, Marl's husband, likes to say that if they had a dime for every time Marl butted into someone else's business, they could buy themselves an ay-rab oil well; but of course they don't have dimes for every time she's butted in and the two subjects in Dolores's life that are truly prime for Marl's opinions are Dolores's marriage to Joe Dean and Dolores's two 'hobbies' – runnin', and photography. *Runnin'* Marl can understand: Senator what's-his-name's a runner there in the Mall in Washington, DC, and so was Jimmy Carter. Turn the TV on these days and all you see is people joggin' all around and workin' out – or better still, go to the supermarket and all you see are people dressed like they're the main event on late night wrestling, even large-boned people, like herself. Well, it's a craze, that's all, Marl thinks, like backyard shelters in the fifties – bomb shelters were supposed to save lives, too, just like runnin' is these days. Next year's life-savin' craze could be artificial wings or sprouted avocado pits – Marl has lived too long to let a temporary fad faze her, but this other thing Dolores does, her 'photography', is genuinely weird: She lays out in the backyard on her back and takes picture after picture of the plain blue sky with a Polaroid color camera. Nothin's on these pictures, not even the occasional bird; just the plain blue sky – but while the picture is still wet, before the yellows and the blues and reds start to appear, Dolores takes her finger and makes squiggly patterns on the surface of it. No two patterns ever come out the same – Dolores says it's because the time element in the chemical film developer is real delicate. Sometimes the patterns come out yellow tinged with orange, and sometimes they come out brown with strange green glows

5

around them. Marl has seen Dolores shoot three rolls of film of ten pictures each in the span of half an hour in a single afternoon. She seems to get herself into a frenzy with the squiggly lines – then she props the pictures up on the kitchen table and stares at them. The ones she likes she tacks up on the icebox door with magnets shaped like cartoon characters. Marl likes pictures that are *of* something. She can't see what these are *of*. If it's squiggly patterns on a shiny little square you're after, she's told Dolores, you could get the same result with a couple tubes of Hazel Bishop and some tinfoil and wax paper and it wouldn't put you out the ten dollars or whatever for a roll of that there delicately fine-tuned film . . .

'Well, come on, Dolores,' Marl declares. 'You gettin' in, or what? I'm not goin' to see you walkin' the Grand Army of the Republic Road at no ten o'clock at night.'

'I'm for a jog, Marl. Actually,' Dolores says.

'Uh-huh. A jog. Then how come I seen you *walkin'*?'

'I was walkin' *fast*.'

'I'll say. You and Joe Dean been playin' at each other's nerves again?'

'I beg your pardon?'

'Come on and pile on in here, girl, before I'm runnin' late. I got to pick up Carl and then we're goin' out to Shoney's for some burgers.'

'Joe Dean *who*,' Dolores asks, like she hasn't heard Marl say anything about the burgers. She settles in the front seat, with her arms crossed on her chest.

'Put your button down on that side,' Marl advises.

'Joe Dean *who*?' Dolores repeats. She stares out the windshield at the long flat road ahead between the soybean fields. Moths are playin' in the foreground near the headlights. 'I don't know nobody by that name,' she says.

'Joe Dean,' Marl reminds her: 'You know, your "Prince Charmin'".'

Dolores rolls her window down a bit and leans her head back

on the seat and sniffs the faint aroma of sulphur in the air. '*She-it*,' she murmurs, à propos of nearly nothin'.

The shifts at the plant where Carl, Marl's husband, works are six a.m. to two p.m., two p.m. to ten, ten p.m. to six – the ten p.m. to six shift bein' called the *graveyard*. The people who pull graveyard are called *stiffs*, or the 'stiff collar works'. The six to two p.m. shift is called *The Nursery*, and the two-to-ten is called *3-T*. That's what Carl's been workin', the 3-T, for six months doin' what he calls *rogue maintenance*. It's plain old maintenance, but Carl calls it 'rogue' because he likes to think since he turned sixty-six it's what he's become. A rogue. A route number. A buccaneer. Marl says, ' "Buccaneer" is right, Carl. *Buck an ear* is what you are: inflated corn.'

Carl tried retirement a year or so ago, but it didn't work. He loves Marl, loves her dearly, but after four dozen years, four dozen summers and winters with one woman it isn't that revealin' or surprisin' to find her there each mornin' nor to climb back into bed with her each night, to say nothin' about a certain lack of invigoration at the prospect of then havin' to have to see her, too, at lunch. Carl likes seein' other things at lunch. He likes bein' 'round young people. He likes bein' around Marl, too – Marl is like old news that's still news, like successive dawns; but young kids are a different kind of news, like storms that wake you in the night from sleeping, like discovering a hornet's nest inside your shoe. Young people are the plumb lines on existence – they let you feel which way you're tilt. Carl likes that. He likes keepin' his brew on percolate. 'Course, he is the first one who'll admit there wouldn't be a thing in him to kindle if it weren't for Marlene having never failed in fifty years to keep his nascent fires stoked:

'Hey, good lookin',' he says to Marl as he comes saunterin' across the parkin' lot carryin' his lunch pail and his Thermos. 'How you doin', Marlene?' He reaches in through the window

7

on the driver's side and touches her. They kiss. They are
practically the only old people Dolores has ever seen kiss and
she's disgusted by it. Fascinated, too.

'We got Dolores with us,' Marl allows.

'I can see we do,' Carl says.

'Picked her up on the Grand Army of the Republic Road.
Down by the Beaujeus place.'

'What is it this time, Dolores?' Carl asks, lookin' over at her:
'Same ol' thing?'

Dolores gets a little crook in her neck and says, 'Same ol'
thing, as if it's anybody's business.'

'Hadn't the two of you ought to have the wrinkles on this all
smoothed out by now?' Carl asks.

'Like I said,' Dolores starts to say, but Marl says, 'Push on
over, honey. Carl, get on in here . . .'

'. . . It ain't anybody's business,' Dolores claims, getting a
good whiff of Marl's cologne as she scoots over. It's that bottled
jungle scent that's meant to bring the tiger out inside a man.
Dolores thinks it smells like melon crates set out in the sun out
back a grocery store.

'Well, I think it is our business, Dolores,' Carl says, adjustin'
his relatively long and skinny self before the steering wheel. 'I
think it truly is.'

'Carl's right,' Marlene attests and pats Dolores on the
knee.

'Well, where to, ladies?' Carl asks, flexin' his arms over the
dash: 'Dinner at the Ritz or shakes and fries at Shoney's?'

'Which Ritz, Carl?' Marl asks.

'That one there on Fifth Avenue New York.'

'I think I'd be like to die of brute starvation by the time we
drove all the way to New York City so I say we try our luck at
Shoney's, what do you say, Dolores?' Marl asks.

Dolores hunkers down and puts her feet up on the dash.
'Y'all can just go on and do what you were goin' to do. Y'all
don't need to change your plans on my account.'

'Well, that's real kind of you, Dolores,' Carl says, turnin' back over his shoulder to maneuver in reverse. 'Seein' as we usually pull up on that dirt road just beyond these gates here and French-kiss by the dial light on the radio for half an hour, don't we, Marl?'

'Go on with your smut talk, Carl T.,' Marl admonishes. 'Just go on with it.' She puts her head down on his shoulder while he drives, and rubs his leg. 'You feelin' all right, honey?' she asks a bit more softly.

'A little tired,' he admits.

Out Route 10 a ways, beyond the overpass, Carl makes a left-hand turn onto Bermuda Hundred Road. He likes this bypass road 'round the town because the town, this time of night, is frankly depressin' – streets all emptied out and every other store all boarded up. The railroad used to run right through the center of the town right across the main drag by Vegari's Cleaners, but the railroad doesn't choose to come through, anymore. Re-routed or abandoned, the big ol' locomotives and the miles of hummin' tracks are gone from bein' everyday occurrence in Carl's life. A lot of what he thought of as a boy is all tied up with railroads. Conrail maintains this line along Bermuda Hundred Road and Carl can sometimes hear a freight horn and catch a glimpse of the old names – Chattanooga, Roanoke, Durham, Tuscaloosa, Chesapeake. Carl saw his first CN rolling stock while standin' in a field adjacent to this very road, when he was five or six years old. He was standin' with his Daddy and his Daddy said out loud, ' "*Portage la Prairie, Manitoba.*" "What?" I said,' – Carl's tellin' Marl and Dolores the whole story; Marl's already heard it countless times: 'Then he said, "Oh, nothin'," and just stared after that freight like he had lost somethin'. "*Portage la Prairie*" – I remember that just sounded all like some kind of jumble, but I looked it up and there it was this little dot way up by a blue lake in Manitoba, Canada. I remember I said later, "Daddy, has you ever been up there in them wild Canadian woods?" and he

9

turned 'round and looked at me as if I'd no sense whatsoever at all. I guess he knew I knew he hadn't of been. Still, I think I'd hoped he had. Do you get what I'm sayin', Dolores? I truly believe we all have one place that we think about. One place on the map. To my mind, I think of Daddy in his Heaven and my thoughts go zingin' up to that little dot by that blue lake on the map. How 'bout you?'

'How 'bout me what?' Dolores answers.

'Where's your own place that you think about?'

'I don't. I don't think about such things,' Dolores says.

'Of course you do, Dolores,' Carl insists. 'Marl here thinks about Ta-hiti all the time, don't you, Marl? Ever since she saw some Marlon Brawlin' movie. Tell her, Marl.'

'I like them say-rongs and those big red flowers in their hair and eatin' with my fingers,' Marl confesses. 'And it was that Paul Gaugwon that did it for me, not no "Mutiny" on no "Bounty" movie,' she reminds her husband. 'Marlon Brando. Go on,' she says, shaking her head. 'You know I never took to beefy men.'

'Except Wallace Beery,' Carl reminds her.

'Well, *Wallace Beery*, Carl . . .'

'Uh-huh.'

'He reminded me of Pops . . .'

'Uh-*huh*,' Carl says, again.

'I guess I do,' Dolores volunteers, 'I guess I do have a place I think about. I don't think of it as Heaven, though,' she says. 'I just think about it. And then sometimes when I find out I'm thinkin' about it, it comes as a surprise, and I try to stop it.'

Marl says, 'That's the same with me with thinkin' about Death, Dolores,' but before her meanin' has a chance to really settle in, they all see this little foreign car pulled off on their side of the road with its headlights blinkin' and a big ol' sparkly sticker stuck in its back window that says, 'Please Call The Police'. Carl, slowin' up the Dodge, says, 'What the hey is *this*?'

He brings his foot off the accelerator and comes parallel with the stopped car and there's a woman sittin' in the driver's seat starin' out ahead.

'Maybe they got these volunteers drummin' up the po-lice business since the rate of crime has fallen off throughout the nation,' Marl submits.

'I think her car has broken down,' Carl says.

He pulls ahead a little onto the clay beside the road.

'Dolores, hand me that there flashlight in the glove compartment,' he requests.

As he says this, the woman in the car behind them turns on her high beams and a wicked stroke of light reflected in the Dodge's rearview mirror hits Carl in his eyes.

'Lordie,' he maintains, 'what does she think we are, a flyin' saucer?'

He gets out the driver's side and Marl shoves out behind him and he walks over to the car and knocks on the lady's window. 'Hey, there!' he calls. 'What's the trouble?'

Without turnin' to look at him, the woman shouts, 'Please, get back into your car, sir! I've written down your license number. Please, just report my disabled vehicle to the State Police.'

'Why?'

'What?'

'Why have you writ down my license number?'

'Please, if you want to help just call the State Police!' the woman shouts through the closed window.

'What's she sayin', Carl?' Marl calls from a distance.

'Damned if I can get it straight,' Carl answers.

Marl comes over to the car and raps against the window. 'Shine the flashlight on our faces, Carl, so she can see us – Hi! We're just plain folks! You in trouble in there?'

The woman turns and looks at them with an expression of mild disbelief.

'I think she's frightened, honey,' Marl says, and she hollers to Dolores: 'Dolores! Get on out of the car and come on over here!'

'I'll bet she'll roll the window down and talk to Dolores,' she tells Carl: 'They look about the same age.'

They step back from the car as Dolores comes over to them and Carl shines the flashlight on the woman's license plate. 'Massachusetts,' he says. 'I should have knowed. Probably one of them Smith or Radcliffe girls. I swear, I think the female brain just fries out on higher learnin' . . .'

Comin' over to them, Dolores asks, 'What's goin' on?' like she has just woked up.

'Talk to this woman, honey,' Marl instructs. 'Ask her what we all can do to help. Carl here has gone ahead and spooked the livin' daylights out of her . . .'

'It's just my native resemblance to your average path-o-logic type,' Carl suggests.

'Back it up,' Marl says and leads him off a ways.

Dolores holds the flashlight in her hand and shines it on the ground in front of her as she walks on over to the car and says, 'Evenin'. You all right in there?'

The woman turns her head and stares right at Dolores.

'My name's Dolores,' Dolores says. 'Aren't you hot in there? I don't see how you can breathe with all your windows rolled all shut like that . . .'

The woman rolls the driver's window down a crack. 'Are those your parents?' she asks, nodding toward the couple in her headlights.

'Them?' Dolores asks. 'Oh, no, they're just Carl and Marl. They're my landlords. Well, actually, Marlene's my husband Joe Dean's landlady. Carl and I aren't on the lease. Where're you from? Are you out here on your own?'

'My car is stalled.'

'Oh, Carl'll fix it,' Dolores says.

'Carl?' The woman asks uncertainly.

'I told you,' Dolores prompts: 'That's Carl and that's Marl.

12

My name's Dolores. Joe Dean, that's my husband, and I rent from them. They're real nice people . . . Carl!' she calls. 'This lady's havin' trouble with her car –!'

'Like we couldn't figure that'un out ourselves,' Carl mutters to Marl as he walks over to the woman's car. He takes a deep breath before he speaks, and a scent of honeysuckle mixed with ditch water floods his senses. 'How do, m'am,' he says, nodding his head sharply. 'What's the problem?'

She rolls her window down an inch or two.

'My car won't start,' she says.

'Just died out on 'ya, did it?'

'Yes.'

'Didn't overheat or nothin' first?'

'No.'

'Well, how many cylinders this got?'

'Four.'

'Geez, if they ain't sold this nation on ponypower I don't know what . . . You got a hood latch in there?'

'Yes.'

'Well, open up the hood, honey, let's take a looksee on the inside,' he advises.

'I'm not your "honey",' the woman says.

'Everyone's my "honey",' Carl informs her.

He smiles this little thin-lipped smile like he's tryin' to play music with a piece of paper and a comb, and he says, 'Try to start her up again when I give you the signal . . .'

He goes forward, raises the hood and has Dolores shine the light in there.

'Where you from?' Marl asks the woman, meantime.

'What?'

'Whereabouts are you from in Massachusetts?' Marl asks more distinctly and at a decibel accommodating to the slightly deaf.

'Oh. Cambridge,' the woman answers.

'Oh, I know where that is,' Marl mentions, proudly. 'Right

outside there of Boston. Carl and me lived a bit in Belchertown, you know where that is?'

'What? No.'

'Out there near South Hadley. You know where South Hadley is?'

'No.'

'Amherst, then,' Marl says, a little piqued. 'Do you know where *Amherst* is?'

'Oh, sure,' the woman says.

'Sure,' Marl nods in agreement. 'College town. Figured you'd recognize a college town . . .'

'Fan belt's broke!' Carl calls.

'What?' the woman asks.

'You have to shout for her, Carl, she's hard of hearing,' Marl calls to him.

'Fan belt's broke!' he repeats.

'Your fan belt's broke,' Marl tells her.

'I *heard* him,' the woman says.

She gets out of the car and Marl steps back. She's just a little thing, Marl observes, built a good deal like Dolores but with a lot more fancy trim work. She's got on this shirt like when you see a picture of a great white hunter on safari, and she's got one of those underwater watches strapped around her wrist. She's wearing this little cotton skirt that stops way above her knees and high-heeled sandals with those itsy bitsy pointed heels that leave holes in the clay dirt just like sandworms, Marl notices.

'Is that all it is?' the woman says to Carl. 'It's just a fan belt?' She puts her hands on her hips and peers under the hood.

'Yes, m'am,' Carl says. 'You got another one?'

'*With* me?' the woman asks incredulously. She stares down the road and begins to tap her foot. Nothin' else moves for a little while except the little sparks of light made by the lightning bugs. Finally Marl says, 'Well, I suppose you could ride on into Hopewell along with all of us. Nick's Garage has got to have your kind of fan belt, don't you think so, Carl?'

'Nick'll have it, sure,' Carl says. 'Nick carries every sort of part . . .'

The woman stares into the workings of her car engine and bites her lip. 'No,' she says, 'that's not a good idea. I can't afford to leave the car. I've got my camera equipment in the trunk. And all my cameras . . .'

Dolores's eyes get real bright and she says, 'Your *cameras?*'

'Don't embarrass yourself, Dolores,' Marl forewarns, but Dolores asks, 'Do you take *pictures?*'

'Yes,' the woman says.

By reflex, she hands Carl her business card and he palms it off to Dolores without looking at it.

'"Joyce Davies, Photographer,"' Dolores reads. '*Goll-ee,*' she says.

Marl starts to repeat, 'Now, honey, don't cause yourself embarrassment,' but Dolores cuts in and says, 'I'm a photographer, too!'

'Small world,' the woman answers, dryly.

Carl spits.

'Marl, didn't we know a girl named "Joyce" before?' he ventures: 'Ugly cussed thing with a –'

Marl throttles him with an evil look.

'What kind of camera do you use?' Dolores asks devotedly: 'I use a Polaroid.'

'A Polaroid? Which one? The S-X?' the woman asks, idly.

'The one that costs forty-nine ninety-five,' Dolores answers.

'Look, why don't you just lock your car up,' Carl suggests, 'and ride along with us –' but the woman makes a chopping gesture in the air with her hands held parallel. 'Here's the plan,' she says, interrupting Carl. 'Let's stick to the plan.' They look at her. 'I'll stay here and you go call the State Police,' she says. 'I'm not going off with anybody but the State Police.'

Carl picks at his ear with a match and spits again.

'I don't think I want to live in any kind of world where people are so galldang asinine they can't trust no one outside a uniform,' he says.

The woman looks at where he spat, then looks at him and says, 'Well, you're living in it.'

'Well, may be,' he nods. 'That just may be.'

He touches Marl's elbow and they start to walk away.

'Real nice to have met 'ya,' Marl says, mindin' her own manners despite Carl pullin' on her arm.

'Are your pictures in any magazines?' Dolores asks, still lingering.

'Sure,' the woman says.

'Which magazines?' Dolores asks. 'I read "Parade" each Sunday . . .'

The woman starts to get back inside her car and Dolores follows after her.

'Now and then I buy "Newsweek",' Dolores says. 'Sometimes "People Magazine" if it's something that looks good . . .'

The woman slams her car door, then rolls the window down and says, 'You people have no sense of what the real world's really like. Remember that. You live like ostriches. Do you understand? You have no idea what life is really like.'

She rolls the window up.

Dolores blinks. She looks down at the woman's business card she's holdin' in her hand, then she looks at the woman again and says, 'You're not married, are you?' through the glass.

Marl calls, 'Come *on*, Dolores!'

Dolores drags her runnin' shoes over the black round holes left in the red dirt by the woman's high-heeled sandals.

'Give me that there flashlight,' Carl says, when she gets close to him. She hands it over and then Carl, standing by the Dodge, illuminated by the woman's headlights and starin' into them right at her, leans at his waist and rests his chin right on the flashlight beam so his face is lit up from beneath and his eyes look sunk back in his head and his nostrils glow bright orange and his skin looks waxen and then he does his famous lizard imitation at her with his tongue for twenty seconds.

Gettin' in the front seat of the Dodge again Marl says, 'Well, son, I hope that made you happy.'

'Yes, m'am,' Carl attests, easin' the Dodge back onto the road. 'It did.'

They ride a while, wrapped in individual silences like pups inside a bitch until Marl says, 'Livin' with this man for fifty years has been one fulltime delight, let me confide that to you, Dolores . . .'

Dolores leans forward in the seat so she can see both their faces and she asks, 'What'd you think of her?'

Carl starts to do his lizard imitation again and Marl lands her elbow in him.

'She had the smallest feet,' Marl marvels. 'Did you see how small her feet and ankles was, Dolores? If I had feet that small I'd be fallin' over on myself the whole time . . .'

'That woman had the manners of saved-over chipped beef at the far back of the freezer,' Carl declares.

'I liked her,' Dolores says.

'Some people like saved-over chipped beef,' Carl observes.

'She was like those women on TV,' Dolores says. 'She was livin' in the real world.'

'Give it up,' Carl murmurs.

'You just didn't take to her like I did,' Dolores says.

'Well, honey,' Carl submits, 'she didn't take to me none, neither.'

Marl shifts a little in the front seat, but Carl keeps real still. Dolores sees his right hand on the steering wheel, near the top of it, real steady. She can see his left arm out the driver's window, perched like it was holdin' somethin' up and for a little bit she almost misses hearing the *tap-tap-tap* he's makin' with his wedding band against the tinplate of the car they're ridin' in.

*

At Shoney's, Home of the Big Boy, out at the Colonial Heights Shopping Plaza, Carl goes straight away to call the County Sheriff from the pay phone about the woman's car, while Marl and Dolores take a booth alongside the plateglass window. Outside, hazy purple shopping center lights buzz with electric current and mosquitoes big as dragonflies, and kids lean up against the cars, listenin' to music. Dolores looks at them and twirls a plastic straw around her finger.

'So what's it goin' to be?' Marl asks, squintin' at the list of burgers and their pictures situated at a place of dominance above the heat lamps behind the counter.

'I don't have no money with me,' Dolores mutters.

'Is that couth?' Marl asks. 'Now is that a couth item of concern?'

Dolores shrugs. 'Maybe I should give Joe Dean a call,' she mentions idly. 'I mean, since everybody's makin' calls.' She makes a tepid gesture with her hand. 'He's prob'ly worried sick about me.'

Marl looks at her real skeptical.

'*If* he noticed that you're gone,' she says.

'He noticed,' Dolores tells her. 'I slammed out.'

'Nothin' broke this time, I hope?' Marl asks.

'Nothin' *broke*, Marl,' Dolores answers moodily.

'Same ol' thing?'

Dolores nods and looks out at the kids and cars lined up in the parkin' lot. 'Same ol' thing,' she drawls. '"Pack it all in. Live out in the woods".' A burst of laughter rises in the distance. 'I ever tell you what his momma says?' Dolores asks, lookin' back at Marl.

Marl shakes her head.

It never occurred to Marl Joe Dean might have a momma.

'His momma says they should had blown the whole place up, themselves included, 'stead of comin' home,' Dolores says.

'Sounds like his momma has a heart a' gold,' Marl mentions.

'Even so . . .' Dolores shrugs.

She looks at Marl and says, 'The nightmares.'

'*Still?*' Marl asks.

Dolores gives her the kind of look that could wilt lettuce.

'You'd think that after ten years –' Marl says.

'Eleven,' Dolores corrects. 'He's been back eleven. We'll be married exactly ten years this September.'

'Ten years,' Marl repeats.

Dolores sees Marl thinking, 'And you still don't have no kids,' so she looks away. Everybody thinks the same around here. That's what really gets her. They all think she's some kind of deviate because she don't have kids. 'You can go to hell with what you're thinkin', Marl,' she says.

She wraps the plastic straw around her finger tight enough so it looks like it will pop.

'You watch your mouth, Dolores,' Marl warns. 'It wouldn't kill you now and then to pretend you was a lady. 'Specially in front of Carl.'

'Is that what *you* do, Marl?'

Marl runs her thumb underneath her bra strap where it's digging in her shoulder.

'Child,' she answers, 'let's put some carbohydrates on your stomach. Your brain's in need of sugar additives. What you goin' to get to eat?'

'Nothin'.'

'Have some barbecue of beef and fries.'

'I don't want it, Marl.'

'And a Colossal Shoney Shake.'

Dolores gets this pinched look 'round her eyes.

'Or do you want a Coke with that?' Marl asks. 'Dolores?'

She hates it when young people cry. It makes her feel all nursey.

They are ridin' out the old Bermuda Hundred Road when Carl gets goin' on the subject of this Shug McPherson who Marl says she can't stand to look at anyway since Shug went and peroxided half her hair. 'You won't remember this, Dolores,' she says, 'but Shug had raven-colored hair. Raven-colored, weren't it, Carl? I would have traded in my teeth for hair that shiny. From the back she used to look exactly like Liz Taylor, didn't she though, Carl?'

'Well, maybe. Sittin' down,' he says.

Dolores could care less about Sugar McPherson.

'Let's drive past and see if the police has come to help that Massachusetts woman,' she directs.

Carl makes the turn onto the bypass road and says, 'Only in human bein's do you find one generation turnin' on the next. You don't find that happenin' elsewheres in nature. It's unnatural. Peanut babies don't turn heel in the field and run off to be walnuts. People ought to take their daddy's lives into account before they run right out and vote Republican.'

'Now don't let's get goin' on Shug and her daddy. Let's let our food digest,' Marl tells him.

'I should have whupped her.'

'The day you whup a woman is the day I set you free,' Marlene declares.

'Are you tryin' to tell me Sonny McPherson lived and died just so's his daughter could peroxide her hair and trot around Shoney's at ten thirty on a week night in designer jeans?' Carl asks.

'Which was a size too small for her, if you ask my opinion,' Marl sniffs.

'Is that what you're tryin' to tell me, woman?' Carl demands.

'Oh, lay off it, Carl,' Marl says, beginnin' to sound peeved.

Dolores has never seen them bicker with each other.

'What's so bad about this Shug McPherson, anyway?' Dolores asks.

Marlene heaves a sigh. It sounds like someone's blowin' up a beach ball.

'I should had brought along a magazine if I'd have knowed I'd have to listen to all this,' she maintains.

'Shug McPherson has growed up to hold tight to strong beliefs,' Carl answers. 'And there's not a one among them that ain't *wrong*.'

'Says you,' Marl murmurs.

'And she's teachin' little kids in school,' Carl says. 'Marl and me worked with Shug's momma and daddy before they died, back in the fifties and sixties when people were still ignorant enough around these parts to deny their laborers the right to vote. So after Marl and I came back from livin' up in Massachusetts for a while, I run smack into Shug McPherson out at the U-Krops one day when I was buyin' rubber hose and she says, "Why, hello, there, Mister Tanner," like she's surprised to see that I ain't dead, "What are you doin' with yourself these days?" "Nothin'," I say. "I'm retired. How 'bout yourself, Shug?" She says, "Oh, I'm teachin' school," so I says, "Well, that sounds like a challengin' and interestin' career, maybe I'll come by some day and give a little talk," and she says, "Oh, would you? That would be so darlin'. You could show them pictures of New England," so I say, "How's this Friday?" and she says, "Friday would be wonderful." So Friday I show up and here's this roomful of all these kids nine and ten years old dressed up like for Halloween. "What's goin' on?" I says to Shug. "Oh, today's the day that they're dressed up like people in their storybooks," Shug says. "Oh, yeah?" I say. "Well who's *he*?" There's this kid no more than nine years old turned out in full gauge jungle camouflage. "Who are *you* supposed to be?" I ask him. "I'm G.I. Joe," he tells me. "The hell you *are*," I tell him. "*I'm* G.I. Joe. I'm the *original* G.I. Joe. I'm the first G.I. Joe they ever made. You're just a little boy." So he shows me his knife. This little boy has got a knife. So I look at Shug and Shug inspects the she-lac on her fingernails. So I says, "What are you doin' with that knife, son?" and he says, "You can't go nowheres in Hopewell without a weapon." The boy is nine or ten, now, Dolores, do you understand? And then point blank in the classroom he says, "Because of all them niggers," while the aforesaid Miss Young Sugar McPherson is just standin' by countin' on her fingers and her toes how many days to go until summer vacation . . .'

'Hey, stop a minute, this is where she was,' Dolores says all of a sudden.

'Pull over, Carl,' Marl tells him.

Carl pulls the Dodge over to the shoulder of the road and turns the motor off.

After a bit he turns the headlights off, too.

'She ain't here,' Dolores says.

'We all can *see* she ain't,' Carl says.

He rolls his window down.

'I guess the County Sheriff came and got her towed while we were sittin' down at Shoney's,' Dolores says.

Marl says, 'It's almost like she wasn't here at all.'

'I wisht I'd talked to her some more about photography,' Dolores says.

'Carl, roll your window up,' Marl says, 'I'm getting bit to death by these mosquitoes.'

'Shh!' Carl whispers.

He opens the car door and gets out.

Dolores sits real still.

The night is full of what Joe Dean insists are jungle sounds.

'What's he doin'?' Dolores whispers, twistin' in the seat a little.

'He hears somethin',' Marl explains.

Dolores listens.

'Joe Dean hears things, too,' she whispers.

'Choppers,' she tells Marl.

Carl has walked across the road and back again and now he leans his reedy face down through the window and says, 'Come on out here, girls. We're in for a real treat in a minute.'

They follow Carl across the road and stand a little ways into a field that's been let go, but which used to be rotated in and out with beans and sorghum. Crickets and night peepers are makin' overlappin' noises. Dolores feels her ankles prickle in the scrub.

'Was that true, what you said about you were the original G.I. Joe?' she asks.

They're standin' there, just waitin' in the dark for God knows what.

Carl has his arm around Marl's shoulders.

'I reckon,' he says.

'Was you in the War?' Dolores asks.

'I was.'

'Did you shoot somebody?'

'Yes.'

'Did you kill them?'

'Yes.'

'Did you shoot them from the air?'

Dolores sees Marl tug a little on him, 'round his middle.

'No, I never did, Dolores,' he says quietly.

The train comes rollin' by.

Not even Marl can count the cars.

They pull up by the drive, where they can see the light on in the bedroom.

'Well, thanks, y'all,' Dolores says.

She remembers somethin'.

'I didn't bring anything from Shoney's for Joe Dean.'

'Here,' Carl says. 'Joe Dean can have this.'

'This is just a shakes lid,' Dolores says about it, turning it around in one hand.

'I threw the cup away,' Carl says.

'But this is just a plastic lid,' Dolores says. 'You can't give a plastic lid to someone and say, "Here, I brought you back something from Shoney's".'

'Why not?' Carl asks.

Dolores stares hard at the two of them.

Finally Marl says, 'Are you goin' to be all right tonight, Dolores? You know we're always just a ways down this-here road.'

'I know,' Dolores says.

Marl plants a wet one on her cheek and Dolores waits 'til Carl has pulled the Dodge out of the drive before she wipes the inside of her forearm across her face where Marlene kissed her.

She goes up the cinder drive.

She's quiet comin' in.

There's hardly any light at all that comes into the kitchen from the bedroom, just a slanted harsh rectangle of it falling on the floor and up one wall behind the kitchen table where her Polaroids are spread out. In the dim light they look ghostly, washed of color, like plain wisps of smoke, or steam escaping from a puncture – tens of them, or even hundreds, she must have taken several hundred pictures of the sky by now, making startling figures in the finished products just by tracing her own fingers in the chemicals. He calls to her:

'Is that you, baby?'

She answers moodily.

'It's me.'

'Where you been?'

'Ridin' 'round with Carl and Marl. We went out to Shoney's.'

'Out to Shoney's?'

'Yeah.'

'Did you get somethin' to eat?'

'Not really.'

'Did you bring me somethin'?'

She looks real carefully at one of the ten Polaroids she shot this afternoon.

It says something, very nearly.

It very nearly says what she imagines it was like.

'Baby?'

He's standin' in the doorway, shirtless.

'Did you bring me somethin' home?'

She shoves her hands behind her, turning 'round the edges of the plastic lid between her fingers.

'What did you bring your lover, baby?'

The light behind him makes the skin along his back and shoulders look like he's on fire.

'What did you bring me home, Dolores?' he repeats.

Imagine turning 'round and looking up not seeing any faces just some rockets shooting through you.

'This,' Dolores says.

Stonewall Jackson's Wife

Hetty comes through the scroll-cut oak door into the summer kitchen with the cold ash pallor persons of her color manifest when they remember how they fear a mutilation more than they fear death, and she says, 'Ol' Jack been shot at.'

Davis, standing at the dry sink doing beans, says, 'Ol' Jack always have been shot at.'

'He has took it this time,' she laments, and then she wipes her hands among the folds of her white apron. Where in wartime have the womenfolk of Richmond found their ample cloth for starched white servants' aprons, except to take the tuck-up off their sheets with sewing scissors or to go out begging under pretense to their neighbors: 'Our boys are in such dire need of bandages,' I've heard Miss Anna pleading. 'Have you anything to spare? A sheet? A drapery lining – ?'

'Oh, they has sent Cap'n Joe to fetch Miss Anna,' Hetty says,

29

perspiring. She sits, as I draw nearer. 'He has bought his ticket this time, Lord have mercy on his soul. Ol' Jack has fine'ly bought it.'

'Hesh,' Davis demands. 'Don't want to know this,' he insists. He walks to where I stand and looks at Hetty. He seems at least a hundred. Even I, whose senses are impaired, can smell the age on him, like brown leaves underneath a snow, the aroma of decay, of dirt.

'How bad he hurt?'

'He gone.'

'How bad?'

'Joe say they did have cut Jack's arm right off.'

'Which one?'

'Joe say Jack cry out, "Oh, Lord in Heaven! My own men – !"'

'Which arm they's talkin' 'bout – ?!'

'The left, I thinks.'

'Oh, Lord. Oh, Lord our Son and Father. They has cut the hand the closest to our master's heart.'

They weep.

I heard them thinking, 'What Fate will I encounter now? What artificial loyalty must I now evince?'

I think all bats are former slaves. I think a bat that flies into a person's face in a locked room is slavery gone to its black heaven. I told Jack that once and I could see he thought my soul was in an awful danger; but he wanted me. He wrote his sister I was like his self, his kindred spirit, he wrote: 'Tell Miss Eliza that she might be on the lookout for something in relation to myself, when she meets Eleanor.' We were like-halves. Like-halves. We were Polarity. A weighted force in Nature, like spring. Like lust. A monsoon. A mistral . . .

Miss Anna's in the front room by the dusty street and her brother, Captain Joseph Morrison, is on his knee beside her.

His sheathed, outdated saber presses down upon the faded carpet, seems to anchor him. How many men have been run through to their deaths by sabers in this war – a dozen? Fifty? Seven hundred? Look at him kneeling here, gold bands of light falling on his face through slatted shutters. I told Jack once these sabers were the stays and crinolines of the Southern officers and he did not appreciate the disrespect I'd shown toward decorative weaponry. I never took too seriously the philosophy of war, it seemed a carnal prospect. Try as I may I could not understand the honor men bestow on taking arms, and fighting. I do smell it now, the war. Its fatigue and dissipation scents the dust that hangs above Captain Morrison's distress on narrow golden bars of mourning light. I smell war and I see it. Jack could not have guessed that it might come to Richmond. Richmond! Jack, who fell in love with Paris. Jack, who fell in love with Boston, Montreal, New York, Washington. Jack, who as a young man, pledged to me, 'All I am and have, I give you.' Jack, who then wrote, when he'd married Mary Anna, 'All I am and have is at the service of my country.' Jack, who stood before the Southern youth at VMI that spring and shouted, 'The time may come, young gentlemen, when your state will need your services, and if that time comes, draw your swords and throw away your scabbards!'

Jack.

Stonewall.

In the North, they use your name to frighten children.

'I cannot bear it!' Mary Anna cries. She has the nervous gestures of intelligence, but her wit is not original. She learns by rote. She is a lumpy brown-eyed girl, not pretty. Her mouth is crooked and her face defies a symmetry. When she is crying, which she often is, she's positively ugly.

'We must leave as soon as possible,' her brother says. 'Lee has sent a train and I've orders for a garrison.'

'But what if we're attacked – ?' she cries. Then, 'No, no, of course, I need to go at once to our dear husband –'

Oh, how this Anna does amuse me: she is forming now the plots and postures, to say nothing of a wardrobe, of a noble general's wife. In her empty-headed way she will call on God more often than is morally acceptable (*God* will choose his final suit of clothes, *God* will help her curl his hair in death before the general staff may view him, *God* will guide the hand of a sculptor named Zamboggi who'll apply the plaster of the death mask). Anna will faint tomorrow in the presence of his body on the camp bed. She will grow impatient with the wait she must endure until he finally dies, five days from now, on Sunday. She will have no courage, none, to tend his oozing wound or to wonder, even for a moment, where his disciples buried Jack's poor, fated arm. She will not remarry and she'll go quite mad, as Jack did, when his first wife passed away.

In the shaded room above the garden, upstairs, baby Julia lies sleeping underneath a cotton mesh ententment, scented through with wisteria and rosewater. Her breathing's light and even, and her little eyelashes quiver in her dreams. She is a perfect blossom of a child – sturdy, healthy, dark-haired, with an even temper and relaxed comportment in a stranger's arms. They named her Julia, to honor Jack's own mother. Their first child, Mary Graham, died when she was two weeks old, from jaundice. Hetty and I both knew that she would. Hetty had told Miss Anna she must squeeze the baby's nose the third day after birth and if there followed yellow streaks across the baby's cheeks, then it was certain she had jaundice. Hetty is Miss Anna's chattel from the family home in North Carolina. She was Miss Anna's nurse. 'I'll do no such thing as squeeze my baby's nose,' Miss Anna said, 'that's like to suffocate an infant.' So Hetty and I met in baby Mary Graham's room and pinched her little nose and when Anna discovered us, she shrieked out loud. Old Jack was downstairs in his study, this having been in '58, when we were still in Lexington. Mary Anna came into the room, straight from the birthing bed. It was the first time, since the childbirth, she had walked and I beheld her with some awe. Her hair, her dull brown hair was all afright, and she was in her muslin nursing gown. I could see she was not right, somehow, that something was amiss: I flew to Jack. Hetty, in the way that coloreds have of talking half out loud their chief and native thoughts, said, 'Hol' still, baby,' both to me and Anna – but I was gone. I flew downstairs to Jack, this being evening. It was then I finally felt how things had gone:

I'd heard it said that he had taken up the habit of an hour's meditation every evening, in addition to his free admission that his day was spent in almost constant prayer. So concerned was he with prayer, or so consumed by need of it, that he felt constrained not to eat nor take the simple time to swallow. He, who so often in the past had shared a plate of oysters with me, or had bitten teeth into a spoon of beaten cream, would eat bread only, with a little milk, and berries. He was obsessed with matters of his health: he stood while reading, or while writing, at a high desk with no chair, so that he might conserve the perfect alignment of his organs. He abstained, all of a sudden, from all drink. He was convinced that one side of his body was more weighted than the other and he disciplined himself to sleep and to sit horseback with his arm extended to correct the problem. He had suspicions he was party to a strange disease. On their honeymoon both he and Anna took the cure of baths. They went to springs at Brattleboro, in Vermont, and at Northampton, Massachusetts. He began a regimen called the Round Hill Water Cure, and when they returned to Lexington he left Anna there to augment his own program with a sojourn at White Sulphur Springs. He became increasingly eccentric; known to suck on lemons, six or seven, through the day. At Manassas, at Fredericksburg, at Harper's Ferry, and at Slaughter Mountain, he was seen, sucking a lemon. No one

33

knew how Jack obtained them, in the midst of war; but, indeed, he did. He would not read by artificial light, neither lantern nor a candle. At war, an adjutant was free to ruin his own eyesight, reading the dispatches to Old Jack, while Jack sat, eyes closed, in a chair. At home, in Lexington with Anna, he would sit in evening 'reading pages in my mind,' his chair pulled up to face the empty wall; and so I found him.

'Jack!' I urged.

He would not move.

'Jack!'

I pushed at him, but could not rouse him.

I flew upstairs.

It seemed to me that Anna was about to strike at Hetty.

'Don't do it!' I shouted in Miss Anna's ear. She drew her arm back and flung it flat against the colored woman's head. I said to Hetty, 'Hit her back!' Miss Anna clutched her breast then, as if she were in pain. She teetered on her legs. 'It's nothin', baby,' Hetty said. 'It's just that mother's milk that comin' down that's causin' all that pain.' Anna's eyes grew very bright. She cupped her left breast in her hand and I could see the start of a dark wetness on the muslin near her nipple. 'Oh, Lord, give me the strength to do Thy deeds,' she wept. She struck Hetty once more, against her head, snatching with the fingers of her other hand at her own breast. 'Oh, ecstasy!' she cried. 'Oh, ecstasy in Thine own holy work!' The savagery, such as I witnessed, went on and on with Anna beating Hetty, until that mean and ugly girl exhausted all her weak and perverse pleasure. I flew to Hetty and consoled her, 'There's a white hell somewhere for these girls.' I went to Anna, and I threatened, 'Jack and I took pleasure in our bodies, yes! we used to suckle on our sins –' But I knew I didn't want him, anymore. I did not know yet what I wanted, but it wasn't Jack. It wasn't Jack, and it was not the life that Stonewall Jackson's wife was living . . .

*

34

Thomas Jonathan Jackson, Lieutenant General, CSA, accepted three musket wounds into his upper body on the evening of May 2, 1863, a Saturday, near the field of battle known as Chancellorsville, in Virginia, from two frightened boys of the Eighteenth North Carolina by the names of Stuart Dixon and Bob Smith. The first and least significant of these wounds lodged a musket ball in his right hand – a smooth-bore Springfield bullet, which identified the weapon which had fired on him as having come from his own men. A second musket wound, more serious, had made its entry at his left elbow, passed through his forearm and emerged above the inside of his wrist. The third and final wound had passed into his left shoulder, torn the shoulder muscles, and fractured his collarbone. It was this final wound that bled most freely. In addition, his beloved mount, whom he called Fancy, had wheeled and reared and carried Jack into the brush, where he was stunned unconscious by a branch. He lost his cap, and Fancy took to Federal lines, from which he was returned to add a depth of meaning, riderless, at Old Jack's funeral.

Within a few short hours of the shooting, in the dark and in the panic of the battle, they collected him along a road into an ambulance. They fed him, in this order: whiskey, morphine, whiskey, chloroform (at surgery); and coffee, afterward, to bring him 'round. He said that while they'd had him under, he'd imagined he'd heard music; then he said he guessed that what he'd heard had been the surgeon's saw.

On Sunday morning – a clear day, and cool at breaking – Jack himself dispatched Joe Morrison from the field hospital behind the lines to come to Richmond for his sister Anna and for the baby Julia. It is Tuesday, though, before Joe reaches us; and Tuesday Jack is moved farther south, by wagon, to a planter's house called Guiney's Station on the Fredericksburg & Richmond Railroad Line. That night he calls for cold wet towels to be applied along his chest and stomach, a remedy of his own device against whatever makes him sick. 'It's Life that

35

sickens you,' I whisper. In spirit, I've already flown to him.

It's Thursday mid-day when our train arrives. Loblolly pines, top-heavy, line the railroad tracks; arbutus thrives along the path beneath the hooves of horses. As always, amid real sights, real sounds of any Army, I am sick at heart from lack of understanding why a form with death as its one substance must persist with so much spectacle as if to say, 'Be happy you may kill your brother, Be proud you can observe the rules of a forced march.'

I fly among the Volunteers kept hidden from our party beyond the hill at Chandler's house, the wounded stretched on filthy oil-cloths outside the slave barracks, and I whisper, 'Now! Desert! Desert –!' but they won't hear me.

As we enter from the wooden porch of the white cabin where Jack lies, I sense Anna will buckle: this is not what she expected. She is wearing her slate-grey-and-loden velvet with its natural peacock feather and the men about are shoddy and foul-smelling. Jack's asleep, and Anna faints away, at sight of him. Reviving her, we try again – Anna, Hetty with Miss Julia, and Mrs Hoge, Anna's traveling companion for the trip from Richmond. A full complement of Jack's staff officers is here, and Doc MacGuire, Dr Coleman from the old division, Surgeon Walls, and Reverend Lacy. There is little fresh air in the tiny room. We watch and wait, and finally Jack stirs. I am over by the window that looks out on the well outside, near some subalterns with fixed bayonets, and Hetty. Jack moves his head from side to side and wets his lips, his eyes still closed. All of a sudden his blue gaze opens full on Anna and his eyes light up as she steps forward.

'Elly!' he cries, joyfully.

His head sinks in his pillow and his eyes fill up with tears.

'My darling Eleanor,' Jack cries and reaches out his only hand.

An awful silence falls, as swift I fly among the men requesting, 'Ask who Elly is.'

A voice, near Anna, asks, 'Who is this Eleanor –?'

I fly among the back-row men and tell them, 'Mrs Jackson.'

'Old Jack's former wife,' a person says.

I stay among them, filling them with things to say:

'She dead?'

'They married?'

'What's her name?'

'She dead –?'

'Oh, Lord, an awful tragedy,' is heard.

Anna churns her arms about her, as if falling, but she doesn't fall.

'Oh, air! More air!' she shouts.

'Eleanor!' Jack calls.

'His first wife,' someone explains.

'Louder!' I implore.

'She died in childbirth,' someone volunteers. 'Their son, the General's son –'

'Born dead!' somebody else announces.

Without my even prompting it, we are treated to the words, 'You know, I heard she was a Yankee . . .'

Jack dies on Sunday, at three-fifteen that afternoon. The staff attending cannot help but notice that his wife, a ready widow, has grown short with him by then, impatient. At three-seventeen she swoons upon the porch, for all to see and to record; but at four o'clock she is at his death bed with a jar of fresh pomade, arranging Old Jack's final hair. Before his officers are let in, she has changed into her widow's weeds (which she has packed), and has inquired of a Captain

37

Wilborne to procure for her a brand new suit of clothes in which the General might be buried; and an artist, an itinerant, if necessary, to take Old Jack's death mask. She allows it to be written, in a dispatch to Lee, that Jack's last words have been, 'Allow us to cross over to the far side of the river and rest forever in the shade of our Lord's tree.'

Our funeral party leaves for Richmond early Monday, on a private train. There has been no new suit that's fit for Old Jack found among the officers, and so he's fitted out in old civilian woolens from the plantation master's wedding trunk at Guiney's Station. His coffin is Virginia pine. Around his head the men have strewn whatever could be cut: wild grass, arbutus, pitcher plant, blue flag, and tulip. A perturbing message comes to Anna from Lee, stating he cannot afford to spare the Stonewall Brigade to march at Old Jack's funeral. I feel she thinks that Old Brigade is gallant, still; I feel her shudder at the ragtag corps that must accompany us.

At Ashland, on the way to Richmond, Anna has her first bad moment, publicly. Women board the train, dozens of them, dressed in mourning, bearing limp road flowers that they've picked for Jack.

'Who are they?' Anna hisses. 'Who are these women?'

'Calm down, baby,' Hetty soothes. 'This the show for all them mothers.'

'What –?'

'This the line of mothers who has lost them sons, along with Mister Jack.'

Anna calls to have the women taken from the train. She is upset by the look of them. But when the engineer begins to move us down the line again, the women stay on board, and we are forced to halt a hundred feet beyond the station. In the dust, then, and the flies, Anna has them put out. 'I do not like that kind of woman,' she confides to Hetty, as she peers at them out the dirty window of the train.

'Well, maybe not,' Hetty admits. 'But it don't mean a thing to them you don't.'

All along the line to Richmond, people crowd the tracks to mourn Old Jack. They are mourning him, but mourning, too, this last lost hope of the Confederacy. At Richmond, the entire city government is mustered out to meet us at the station, and the workers in the city leave their jobs to get a view of his pine casket. A new flag, the one the Congress has intended to raise above the Capitol on Victory Day, is draped on Old Jack's coffin. We march to the Governor's Mansion, and Anna is installed in a large suite, fit for the reception of a king. Tonight, he is embalmed.

All day Tuesday there's a private viewing in the Governor's Mansion and Jefferson Davis comes with members of the Cabinet. There is much weeping up in Anna's rooms, much reading of the Scriptures. It is Davis, though, who is the first to ask if he might pay respects to baby Julia. Anna's mouth is hard around the words, as she acknowledges, 'Of course, you may.'

The next day there is a grand procession down Governor Street to Main, up Main to Second, then from Grace into Capital Square and the Hall of the House of Representatives. We are led by five brass bands, the Nineteenth Virginia Infantry, the Fifty-Sixth Virginia, General Pickett and his staff, six pieces of artillery, and a squadron of the cavalry. The men, appearing strangely refreshed, march with arms reversed. The hearse is drawn by four white horses; Fancy, riderless, is led by a groom, the only Negro in the funeral march, behind the casket. The casket is carried by six Generals into the Hall of the House of Representatives and placed on a white altar rigged before the Speaker's bench, with the colors of the Confederacy still draped over it. During the day more than thirty thousand people come to take a look at Jack. The embalming has been executed with great care and Jack looks much the same as he had in his former life, except his facial features seem much smaller. During the night, Governor Letcher tries to close the Hall to viewers, but a protest goes up among the many lined outside. Three times the Hall is swept of flowers so the viewers will have room to pass. At the Governor's Mansion, Anna receives the many privileged mourners; Virginia politicians and their wives, the City Councils of both Richmond and Petersburg. Many ask to see the baby Julia, longing, apparently, to touch her, especially the men. Finally, near evening, Anna orders Hetty to take the infant to a distant room, until the guests are gone. 'They's no rest for this baby, is they?' Hetty asks out loud, a little later.

Thursday we begin the journey west to Lexington, where ground is waiting for him. The train is slow, so slow that people jump on board with ease and soldiers must be posted on the rails. People line the tracks and crowd the crossroads. They bring flowers and wreaths and call for Anna to receive them. 'The baby!' they begin to shout. 'Baby Julia! Stonewall Jackson's baby!'

'Who are these people?' Anna demands. 'Get rid of them! Tell the engineer we must go faster –'

There is some panic at a rail crossing five miles outside the town of Gordonsville, when a man falls from a wagon onto the tracks beneath the train. When we stop, people throw flowers and bits of cloth against our windows and they clamor for us with their dirty hands. 'Show them the baby,' Anna snaps. She sinks back as Hetty holds the infant to the window. A great resounding cheer goes up, a Rebel Yell.

In Gordonsville the crowd stands twenty deep along the platform and a patchy band plays hymns from the pitched roof of the station. A man in a frock coat, a dignitary, attempts a speech, but the crowd calls, 'Baby! Baby! Stonewall Jackson's baby!'

I whisper to Hetty, 'Hold her from the window. Let them kiss her.'

Hetty says, 'What you think, Miss Anna. Does we want to open up this window –?'

'Yes, yes,' Miss Anna shrinks. 'Do whatever you think best. These people have no sense of decency, no order –'

The window's opened up and Hetty leans her frame over the crowd with baby Julia suspended in her arms. People reach up just to touch her. Fingers poke at her, or smooth her little dress; grey fingers, black with dirt, yellow, red fingers, a gloved hand with a hole along its seam. We pause in Gordonsville for twenty minutes while this ritual goes on, before the train moves west for Charlottesville.

Outside Charlottesville, Anna's overcome with nausea. 'It's the smell of all these people,' she complains to Mrs Hoge. 'I cannot bear it. All this heat. The filth.'

'Of course not, precious,' Mrs Hoge consoles her. She takes Anna's head into her lap and plays with Anna's dull, brown hair.

Soon the crowd outside has slowed us down with calls for Julia. At the station, cries go up once more for Stonewall Jackson's baby and I say to Hetty, 'Tell her we can take the baby out.'

'Miss Anna,' Hetty says: 'Why don't you rest on board the train whilse I go outside with our baby.'

'Absolutely not,' Miss Anna says.

I say in Mrs Hoge's right ear, 'Well, why not, Anna dear? Hetty certainly can do what's best and you would not encounter all these people . . .'

'It's too hot for her,' Miss Anna says.

'I has a parasol.'

Anna sits up.

'Wherever did you get a parasol –?'

41

'I's always have it.'

'You stole it, you mean.'

'For takin' baby Julie in the sun.'

'All right,' Anna relents.

I fly outside.

People all around us shout out, 'Let me see her! Let me touch her! Let me kiss her! Hold her up!'

I go before her in the crowd, gently moving people to the side, both young and old. 'Stonewall's baby,' people murmur. The rank and file close in behind us, in the sun. The people look with wonder on the child and Hetty smiles. 'She don't look nothin' like the General,' someone says. 'Why, she's the little darlin',' someone else begins to say. Far behind us a faint voice cries, 'Hetty? Julia? We need be goin' – *Hetty*?!'

Hetty hands the baby to the crowd. They bounce her up, among themselves. The child begins to giggle.

An old man with brown teeth puts her on his shoulders and begins to jog her all about. 'I had a little pig,' he chants:

'I fed him all on clover . . .

And when he died,

Oh, when he died,

He died, he did,

All over.'

The Gentleman Arms

Only later did she realize it had happened on the summer solstice: longest day, the shortest night. After more than twenty years of wanting to be lovers, she and her old boyfriend meet again for one long day four thousand miles away from home and hold to one another in the shadow of their youth, their lovemaking projects on this, the shortest night of all.

Twenty years! twenty years is one-eleventh of the history of the USA, one-eleventh of recorded history since the birth of our great nation, she attempts to reason. If she and he were two Chinese having been in love for one-eleventh of their nation's sovereign history they would have been in love five hundred years. If they were British they would have been in love for something near a century. Moss would have softened them by now. Their crystals would have gone tar black and wooly through the seasons, instead of this, this instant aging, this

45

quarter of an individual's life. Her old boyfriend! the idea of the two of them together is already born of a cliché: what is one if not cliché throughout one's adolescence, she considers to herself. Not unique. Clearly not original. Incapable of generating melancholy, only heat. Now he's come to England. To find her? she wonders. Up to Wolverhampton to negotiate an import license to sell racing wheels, then down to London to see her, this old boyfriend, this bald cliché gone near-sighted, striding toward the foot of Nelson's column in Trafalgar Square with a walk that hasn't modulated one degree off strident confidence in twenty years, this walk she recognizes instantly, the one that sends her racing through the crowd and calling out his name, these two old kids, these two old rodeo headliners, Annie Oakley and Kit Carson, these two heartbreakers, game but gimpy, eager, loud-mouthed, baffled, loveless, lost and irrepressible; these jokers.

Honey, when did you start smoking?

As if they'd lived together nineteen years and he's come down into the kitchen in his robe for coffee and she's turned around and caught him taking sugar with it the first time. *Marlboro*'s. Well, yes, nothing half-way about William, never will be, never was. If he's going to smoke he's going to smoke the cowboy smoke, the brand that blazes on the dusty trail.

For a moment in Trafalgar Square it seems as if she's seen his figure countless times, it seems as if she's caught his image from the bus, late afternoon in Yorkshire, traversing the dales with that same confidence, the short blade of his scythe bound up in brown butcher paper and black plastic, an anonymous day worker in black leather boots, a cap, a jacket.

'When did I start smoking? When I came back to BOC right after that first mission.'

That's right, she tells herself, we know when we start smoking. We remember when we stop, we start. We remember moments when we fall in love. When someone died. What we were wearing. How she looked.

'What's a "BOC"?' she asks.

'Base Operation Camp. I started smoking and I started drinking Southern Comfort as a ritual the same day I flew my cherry combat mission.'

And I started banging yellow tail, she expects him to add next. And I started raping Oriental women.

'In Viet Nam,' she ascertains.

As if she's calling serves at Wimbledon.

'In F-14's,' he says.

You're kidding.

'From boredom, if you want to know. In between the runs. To pass the time of day.'

You're really kidding.

How many children do you figure you wiped out. How many men. How many women. What do we want from this. Why are you crying. Can we still pretend to love each other in that undeluded way. Can we still pretend each action is significant. That the world may cease or start to be renewed depending on the placement of one's hand inside her skirt, along her back, against her arm, in her brassiere. He remembers the exact surrounding where he finally got her bra off in the woods behind her house on Fordney Road. He remembers everything. She no longer wears a bra. She cannot recall particulars. She does not remember details of specific afternoons. She can't seem to get the band out in commemoration of a victory. His victory. His molars or his milk teeth. His wet dream. His cherry mission. *Bitch.* But does it matter? It doesn't matter, does it? What does it matter? He and she are not in England to commemorate the egg, they're not in England to decide which came first, the grown man or the embryo. They're in England to forget and to remember and to test the threads like tightrope walkers or red spiders: does this hold my darling? What still holds? does anything? We're history's brats, she wants to rant. She's fed up, more than he is, with the pedant's postures, with the forays into longing, with the melancholy shit passed off as substance, with nostalgia, with the rising damp, with Nancy Reagan and her little gun like opera glasses tucked into a beaded bag so cute, so compact, so cosmetic, Christ shut up, he finally tells her, just shut up. Please. Emily. Shut up. Pretend you don't hear water dripping somewhere, just this once.

Twenty years.

Well of course the thing was, after twenty years of waiting to make love, after all the years of waiting to be lovers, after all the time and over all the distance when the moment comes, she's menstruating.

Back then, it would have guaranteed a recognized degree of safety. Now it seems another inconvenience, like the traffic on the roundabout through Epsom, when it's raining. Emily had lost a lease once on a furnished house because she'd stained the mattress, and she'd decided, then, that there are two types in the world, two types of people corresponding nothing whatsoever to the boundary line dividing male from female. There are those for whom the smell of blood lurks inside experience unlocked only by an exercise of all five senses; and there are those for whom the smell of blood, the sight of blood, the drinking, spilling, wasting of it is a mental exercise. One type glamorizes war, and one type sickens of it. One type has its sex its babies and its breakfast in starched white linen rooms; and the other type perspires and says fuckit to discretion. Standing up to get a glass of water, looking down on her across the bed, he says, It looks as if we sacrificed a virgin here. Not funny, she thinks, so she kicks a leg at him. Well, hell. We did, hey, William? I said, hell, we did. Our maiden love affair, our lovely little maidenheads: the girl he never got, the girl he thought he'd lost, the girl he's sought in countless women, meaningless encounters, mangy hotel rooms in foreign countries: let's not make a movie out of this, she whispers. Let's not get heroic. Until you traced me down, until you forced me to remember, up

48

to and including now this very moment, William, you're the boy that I forgot.

We broke up for a while. We broke up for what became the longest while. Do you remember how that happened? Honey? Do you recall why we broke up?
The trouble is, he says, the trouble comes in trying to believe in love. Alright? I love my daughters. I know I love my daughters, that's it. I know what love is, because I know what the feeling is I feel toward them. Ergo, I know what the hell I'm missing when that feeling isn't there, with Barbara, for example. That's the trouble.
'"Ergo"?' she repeats.
'Yes.'
He holds her.
'When did you start saying "ergo"?'
'When I had to learn to rationalize to keep alive. Or maybe when I grew my moustache. Do you like my moustache?'
'Very much.'
She grooms it for him with her kisses.
'It's neat now,' he observes.
'It's very neat.'
'You should have seen it back in Nam. I waxed it.'
'No.'
'I waxed it, fucking handlebar moustachios to here. Fucking combat helmet. Fucking Ray-ban's. Fucking automatic weapon. Fucking ammo clip. Fucking Nasty Dastardly, the dirty dick. Fucking cartoon.'
She watches him, this cowboy. No, she's not going to let this other woman's husband in. This native son. This hotdogger. This race car driver. This marauder. This former major in the Air Force. This jet pilot. This real estate developer. This balding man who loves his children. This man who frequents prostitutes. This man who tells her young girls with great bodies in their twenties don't know how to kiss. This man who whispers

49

things she doesn't want to hear. About her eyes. About the
way her eyes send out a field of green charged with electricity,
the pale green light before an evening summer storm.

'I bet you never thought you'd find me single,' she suggests.

'It didn't make a bit of difference.'

'Well: yes, it does.'

'I didn't care.'

'I mean, it makes this more convenient, don't you think?'

'I wouldn't give a ratfuck whether you were married to the
King of England. I'd show up at the door and say, Excuse me,
fella. Excuse me while I stand here and swallow this woman,
whole.'

But the fact is I'm an old maid. You are not an old maid, I'm
not going to argue with you, Emily. But the point is I live alone.
I live alone while people all around me live together. I'm a
failure. You don't have to *live* alone to *be* alone, he says. Oh fuck
this, everything we say to one another comes out sounding like
an Elvis Presley lyric, anyway.

'Will you be stayin' on another night, Miss Johns?' she's
asked by the proprietress.

'I will, yes. Thank you.'

'With your husband?'

'No. He's . . . he'll be leaving us.'

'Oh, no. Going far?'

'Back to America.'

'Oh, my. I love America.'

'Actually, he'll be wanting you to get a cab, please.'

'A cab? Where to?'

'To Heathrow.'

'Heathrow? He can take the tube to Heathrow.'

'I know he can, thank you, Mrs Cooney. But he doesn't want
to take the tube to Heathrow. He wants to take a cab. He thinks
he'll feel better in a cab. I think so, too.'

Americans and Arabs, that's what Mrs Cooney's thinking, Emily assesses. The next remark will be, Oh well of course, my dear, if money is no object. Wingeing Brits. Why am I going on like this against the native character, against the manners of my home away from home, she chides herself: because of him. Because of his intrusion. Because he's hauled my pedigree, nailed it to the mainsail, made me fact, authenticated me, shown me up for what I am. Defector. An ex-patriot.

'For what time shall I have the cab come 'round then, dear?' she's asked.

'For six o'clock, please, Mrs Cooney.'

'Six it is. Will you be taking tea? There's a cream tea in the garden. Do you think he'd like that?'

'Yes. That would be lovely, wouldn't it.'

Such ease, the cream teas buttressing the spirit, the endless eloquent debates, the proms, the proposition of the weekends in the country. Why did you disappear, he wants to know. The ease, my dear, is lovely; the ease of anonymity, at first. Immersion in a stranger's world. Britain is the same as an old boyfriend for Americans, alright, my dear. Old and strange and still familiar. Don't make light of this, he threatens her. Don't make light of what is going on. What's going on? she asks. Whatever this thing is between us. Oh for christsake, give it up. We would have killed each other, William. Emily, don't kid yourself. We already did.

Was it just us, honey, do you think? Are we just the average product of another generation gone to dust?

'We do love each other,' he insists.

He takes her hand.

Across the garden Mrs Cooney tells another woman, 'He said if I was still in pain he might go fixin' with the spine, but I don't want it. The spines are very tricky, don't you think?'

'Please,' he says, his hands around hers. Come back home. Don't make me lose you twice.

'Some cakes, some strawberries?' Mrs Cooney asks them, smiling. A rare sun breaks the clouds. 'How long have you been married?' Mrs Cooney asks. They stare at her. 'A week? Two weeks?' She serves them thick cream on a slotted spoon. 'I love America,' she tells them. She serves them berries, sugar. 'I have a friend there,' she confides. She passes napkins, flatware, round cakes. 'Really?' William asks. The two of them are dumb, with feeling. 'Yes,' they're told. 'A good friend, actually. A man.' A silence. 'David Barton. Sergeant David Barton. From the War. Could you know him? He's from Illinois.' They look at one another. 'We were very much in love, David and I, back then. Like you two.' Something falls. A breeze starts up. The berries bleed into the cream along their edges on the plates. 'Every time my Davie is in England,' Mrs Cooney says, 'he comes to see me. Tea?' She pours. 'Every time he is in England, Davie drives out here to see me at The Gentleman Arms. Over forty years, you mind. Every time he comes to England. Of course I always give ourselves the best room, every time. The one that you were in. It's special, isn't it? For lovers, isn't it? I save that room for couples like yourselves.'

How many times has David been in England? William asks. He's ready to risk anything. He's holding his old girlfriend's hand in his. And he's in love.

'You mean in forty years?' Mrs Cooney ponders. 'Oh my, oh my, oh my. You mean my Davie? Over forty years? How many times has he been back to stay with me?'

The sun is shining and my heart is young again, my darling.

'That would be, let me see: forty years . . .'

The sun is shining and your hand's in mine, my dearest love, my green-eyed girl:

'Counting the whole time through the War would make it twice.'

And then as if she still can't work it out, she says, 'The War.'

Insomnia

Pete comes back from New York City in September and announces he has accidentally slept with Alice. He says this rather dismally so I don't bother asking, 'Was it good?' Besides I don't believe that people accidentally sleep with one another. Rock Hudson and Doris Day might have accidentally slept with one another in those fifties movies, but no one I know in the eighties accidentally does. Except, apparently, Pete and Alice.

I've heard some people, drinkers mostly, have this kind of experience. But Pete's not much of a drinker. Alice: Maybe. But Pete can't hold his alcohol at all. Two glasses of wine, Pete's under. Sydney Australia is where he might as well be. Or Mars. See, I teach kindergarten so this reminds me: Every year there is this World Unity project in October where every classroom has to deck out like a different country and serve native food and issue border stamps and everybody does these

55

tours around the world in school. My class picked Mars for their country. I mean, out of this world is not beyond belief for them so we all decked out like Martians. There was a problem when it came to what to serve as Martian food and somebody suggested fireflies which I thought was kind of nice but we served sand instead. And walnuts. We're mostly five. There's this one six-and-a-half-year-old I had to keep back from last year. Her name is Phoenix if you can believe. My name is Miss Knight. This time a year ago Pete and I were planning to get married.

What happened? I moved out. I borrowed his station wagon for the move because all my things wouldn't fit inside my sports car. This was six months ago, at the beginning of the summer. I got this place on William Street that has its own garage. It has a butler's pantry too. I guess it was sometime in September I got into the habit of baking things real late at night. It was right around that cold snap.

The things some mothers do: they send their kids to school in freezing weather in these flimsy Orlon sweaters. Every year I see these kids come in, in flimsy sweaters. Please dress your children warmly, I write home. They never listen. So in September I was baking quite a lot. Cookies, coffeecakes, festive breads, you name it. Late at night. It got so bad my freezer wouldn't hold the frozen vegetables. All I had in there were Tupperware containers full of cookies, cakes in plastic wrap. I think at one point I was buying close to three or maybe four dozen eggs and four or five pounds of sugar every week. I was doing this like there was nothing going on in Africa. No starvation. I was doing this as if the world was fine and I had nothing on my mind except baking for a Christmas, or Depression to come round. Then Pete comes back from New York City and announces he has accidentally slept with Alice.

Their names sound good together don't they? Much better than the way it sounds with Pete's and mine. You can just see Pete and Alice in a little cottage by the wood or featured in a sitcom. Much more than you can see two people with the names, Pete and Zorina. 'Pete and Zorina' sound like one man and a snake. Not that Zorina is my name. It's not. It's Geri, short for Geraldine. But you get my drift.

Why did I move out? I guess you have to know me or know Pete or you have to know me when I'm with Pete or you have to know Pete when he's with Alice. Pete and Alice are these long lost friends. They belong to this one bunch of long lost friends from college that you get free when you get Pete. Like something you don't need when you buy soap. Like these teensy tubes of wart removal cream. You wouldn't pay cash money for that kind of stuff but you collect them and you save them even when you move and you end up taking one along on your vacation out of cautionary fear of foreigners. That's what this bunch of friends of Pete's were like. *Are* like. Have always been. Will always be. Like a stuck record.

They talk. I never heard a bunch of people talk so much in my entire life. At New Year's they begin to talk about the coming May, like where they all should summer. In May they talk about their fall ballet subscriptions and the opera. They talk about Thanksgiving. They talk about *what stuffing*. They talk about where they've decided to go they think, with whom, what they might feel like eating maybe, where they probably ought to go to buy their whatzits, how they better start to plan their Keoghs. None of them is married. None has kids. All of them have jobs. Not normal jobs. Not clerkships. Not repairing steam fittings in dank tunnels. No job that comes even close to having to be anywhere on time, on schedule. Fantastic jobs, the most glamorous exotic jobs in the whole universal employee pool. Jobs like buttoning pearl buttons on angora sweaters, one pearl button at a time, just one a day. Or lying down and sleeping for a living. What does Alice do? Writes flaps. There may be three or maybe four flap writers of her calibre in all history. Is this important? Does this matter? What's a flap? Flaps are things that keep the paper dresses up on cut-out dolls.

They keep the cardboard lids on sugar boxes down. They go up and down at great length with great ceremony on the wings of planes before taxiing for take-off. Flaps are eddies of emotions, eddies between humans, small commotions. You can cause a flap. You and I could cause a flap over anything as stupid as a game of jacks but only someone precious brilliant and abiding as our Alice can sit down and *write* one.

Does this make sense?

They put covers they call dust jackets on these books but they never stop to ask the question, Where does dust come from?

About these flaps, see: before you buy a book you look inside and there on the inside of the dust jacket is this nice description of the book on these two *flaps*. Sometimes this description is only on the front flap, but lots of times it's on the front and back along with a picture of the author and a little bio of him. Someone has to write these little descriptions. They're called *flap copy*. Maybe you don't think about this but someone has to write down everything you read. Even stuff that is written on a toothpaste tube. Maybe you don't read these things: on my toothpaste tube it says fights cavities freshens breath even cleans stained film.

What's stained film?

Alice's flap copy never poses these dumb questions. It never makes dumb statements. Editors send her copies of these manuscripts and then she writes the flaps, sometimes four or six flaps in a week. You can always tell her flaps. You can pick up a Russian cookbook or a spy novel or a book on weevil culture and you can tell immediately Alice wrote the flap. She uses favourite words. Her words are 'lambent', 'fresh', 'articulated'.

My words are mostly not inside the English language.

My words are 'fut' and 'dupple' and 'cozmeer'.

I guess I first met Alice when she came to stay the night with us two years ago. This was just around the time Pete and I were telling everyone we wanted to get married. Pete especially was real enthralled with how that sounded. I think for me the way he said it sounded distant. Like next year, you know? Like morning.

What happens is that things accumulate. Like the major question 'Where does dust come from?' It comes from nothing. History comes from nothing. Where does 'time' come from? Where does it 'go'?

It was back when Pete and I were living with each other and we were telling everybody we were going to get married. People still come up to me and say, 'Did you get married?' Do I have that married look? I don't think so. For one thing I talk out loud too much, to objects, to events. When the tire goes flat I say to it, 'Did you have to do this?' When the light at the top of the stairs burns out I ask it, 'Did I need you to do this today?' When Pete tells me he has had an accident and Alice is it I don't say anything. Later, when I'm alone, I say, 'Fine and neat and dandy for the two of them.'

It's funny all the things you can't remember when you want to and then all the things you can't forget even when you try.

Like today I forgot this kid's name.

We were talking in class about grooming, about brushing our teeth and washing our hands and combing our hair and she raised her hand for me to call on her and I couldn't. I looked at her face, at her arm disappearing in her sleeve and I thought, 'I know this kid. I've had her two years. I know this kid's name. I know her parents.'

What she wanted to say, what she finally announced, in fact, when I smiled and nodded at her, was, 'I have *nat-u-ral-ly* curly hair . . .'

Phoenix, that's it.

I forgot it.

And what about things like this: remembering overheard conversations. I mean you'd think you'd forget four people you don't even know in a restaurant. You'd think you'd forget two men and two women too obviously married. What they were wearing: there was a man in a navy blue jacket who was

59

obviously married to the yellow-haired woman in the plaid evening skirt and the hot-pink sweater. There was a man in a grey suit and brown shoes. There was a woman in a white blouse and a black velvet jumper. They were all over-dressed. Their drinks were Manhattans, old-fashioneds and sours. When was this? Years ago. The woman in the hot-pink sweater said, 'Do you know what this one did last week?' to the woman in the white blouse and black velvet jumper: 'He didn't come home.'

'It was after a meeting,' the man in the navy blue jacket explained.

'Says he felt himself dozing off at the wheel and pulled over. Says he spent the night in the car.'

'I'd had a few.'

'Never called. Says he spent the night in the car.'

'In the car.'

'In the car.'

'The whole night.'

'Until morning.'

Why am I thinking of this?

Oh yeah. I didn't believe him.

I mean let's face it no one believed him but everybody said, 'Well, that happens. My goodness, you're not thinking Pete' – (or whatever his name was) – 'you're not thinking Pete's not telling you the truth, are you? Well, my goodness, after all these years? Calm yourself. Pete would never do a thing like that.'

What I should have done – I think a lot about the things I should have done this time of night – I should have walked over to the table and said, 'Pete, you lying dog, why don't you just tell Zorina the truth: You slept with Alice.'

Of course the woman with the yellow hair in the plaid skirt and hot-pink sweater would never have been named Zorina. She might have had a name like Geraldine.

I wish my name were Slim.

There's this woman in the social columns who's always

giving parties whose name is Slim. Can't you just imagine her? That's got to be *some woman.*

It's things like dust, you know? That end up keeping you awake. I don't know, you start to think of all the things you need to do, the things you should have done. And things accumulate. Like I was thinking the other day about its being almost winter and how I used to think that if it weren't for wind the leaves would never fall off trees. I used to think that trees *made* wind. By bending over. They just sort of pushed the wind along.

Sometimes I just remember words I've read. SOLECISM, that's a word. Sol-e-cis-ti-cal-ly. I just think about the word a long long time. I wonder where it came from. How it got to be. Like did you ever think about how people learned the way to eat an artichoke?

I guess being with all those kids makes me 'jejune', sure. I didn't have to look the word 'jejune' up. I knew it. They thought I wouldn't know it, but I did.

Did I say that none of them has kids?

What did I do when Pete gave me his announcement? Hey, nothing. Nothing childish. Nothing. Then I got to thinking one night about this one cartoon. It drove me crazy. See, I'd seen this one cartoon a while back and one night I remembered seeing it. It was in a magazine and it was drawn by that cartoonist who draws vicious looking dogs thin men and portly women without chins. It was this picture, see, of this portly woman with no chin in a hat and overcoat holding her vicious looking dog on a tether on a street corner. The vicious looking dog had most of this milquetoasty looking man's left leg between its teeth. The milquetoasty looking man was staring down at the vicious looking dog and the portly looking woman was saying to the dog, 'Let go of Mr Thurston, Alice.'

Don't you see?

So I got up this one night around three a.m. and hunted through the house for all my magazines and then I sat up in my bed and looked through every one of them but didn't find it. I

looked through every one. This took a long long time. The next
day it occurred to me that maybe I'd seen it in my doctor's office
so after school I drove there and walked in and went through all
the magazines in the waiting room. I didn't care if people stared.
I found it. Tore it right out too and brought it home. It took me
three tries with the scissors one after another to get the edges
straight and then I taped it on a piece of typing paper. I typed
an envelope to Alice in New York and then I folded it all up
and sealed the envelope and glued the stamp exactly straight.
Then I propped it on the dressing table in my room. I was
feeling pretty proud. I was going to get that off the next day, boy.

Then, I don't know, I thought about how stupid it would
look.

I thought about Alice thinking, Who's this Mr Thurston?

So I didn't mail it.

This was back a while ago.

Did I say that none of them has kids?

I think I counted it up one night and I've had five hundred
twenty seven kids. My mother used to count like crazy right
before she died. She loved to count. She'd sit and count the
people in commercials on TV. She'd start to count and then the
picture on the screen would change and she'd just start all over.
Sometimes one two three one two one two. It seemed like she
could never get caught up. I started counting all my kids one
night. I think I got to about five hundred twenty seven but
that's rough. That's really rough.

That's not counting Phoenix twice.

I guess I never thought I'd end up such a classic though, you
know? Like all those Brontë women in those books.

Then one night I got to thinking. It was about three a.m.
Without turning on the light I accidentally called somebody on
the phone. I accidentally dialed her number in New York.
When she answered I said, 'Alice, did I wake you?'

Then I slid the phone receiver in between the sheets where no
one was and I lay very still.

On the Coconuts

We called him the Adoptadon, last of the Key West dinosaurs.

Which was cruel, but funny. The way our women were back then.

We were working on a house out on Katama – Sam the Gram, me, Bumpy and Wise Eddie. We were putting up a house for this boy genius from New York, pulling on his father's friends and all their money, and we treated him like John the Baptist must have treated fair Salome. Righteous. Unmoved. Nothing like your average arrogant asceticism to throw a pall on all that dross of filthy lucre. Oh how we tried to rise above those class distinctions. *Hey your dirty money*, we tried to pretend. While all the while we knew the truth was Hey, our heads.

Adoptadon came by one day while we were digging the foundation and straight out asked, 'Anybody here know a kid calling himself Don Clifton, Junior?' We ignored him. He went away, all right, but then he came back: 'This fella that I'm lookin' for would be, oh, thirty, thirty-five by now,' he claimed.

'Hey what's a five-year spread?' the Gram cracked: 'You sure he's not twenty, forty maybe?'

'What's this guy look like?' Wise Eddie baited him.

'Dark hair, glasses,' the Adoptadon recited: 'Even-tempered. High IQ. Used to own a dog named Nina. Irish setter.'

'How'd he find out about *Nina*?!' Sam demanded in my ear.

'How do *I* know?'

'I mean, *Nina*, man-!'

'My "ex", I guess.'

'The *bitch*,' Sam swore.

'Watcha lookin' for Don Junior for, anyway?' Bumpy asked, because he was born that dumb.

'Oh, he's due to inherit quite a sum,' Adoptadon maintained.

'Is that a fact?' Eddie asked. 'How much, exactly?'

'Well, it's not exact . . .'

'Ballpark,' Eddie allowed.

'Oh, you know,' Adoptadon finessed: 'A sum.'

'A sum of what? Of land? Of money?' Eddie pressed.

'Well, I'm not at liberty to say,' the old man began to hedge.

'A sum of *shit*,' I spat.

We four had work to do.

He might have guessed before, but right that minute the Adoptadon was sure I knew.

The next we heard of him he'd pitched a tent in Corinne's backyard where he was living in it without water. How you meet Corinne: if you're new in town, a little lost, she'll find you. She believes in Mr Right. She wears a button with the slogan 'I Believe in Mr Right' pinned to no matter what she's wearing. She's got a bumper sticker with the slogan on it plastered to her mini-van. Anything you want her to understand you have to say twice because she's always singing the tune *someday he'll come along* to herself, somewhere in there behind her spectacles. *I'd* have given her a look a few years back if it hadn't been for Tracy and for the fact that Corinne's lived alone for more years than I'm old and it shows on her, the way some women show their veins, when you sit down at her table in the coffee shop and she hoards up all the sugar. These women that have fed nobody but themselves for thirty years learn how to hoard up all the salt and pepper and line up all the other condiments as if they were commanding a regiment of *jars*, and then they learn to eat like no one's ever watching. I saw it happen to my mom the Mombo. This world she made. Trying to clasp it all in closer. Like take a big deep breath and hold it. World with a nineteen-inch waist, that's what Tracy called it. Most the things that Tracy ever said like that she took from movies. Like pay no attention to that man behind the curtain. She used to say that all the time when one of her girlfriends came over after work. About me, I mean. She used to say pay no attention to the man behind the curtain about me. And into the garbage chute, flyboy. That was another one. Into the garbage chute, flyboy. To me. From Star Wars. So when Adoptadon pitched his tent in Corinne's yard, Tracy said oh boy just like another my man godfrey. But she didn't know him then. Besides, Corinne's no Carole Lombard.

About Adoptadon: He comes, he stays. You want him out? He stays. You let him use your phone, you got yourself a houseguest. Once he actually got married. This was way back when. He married this nice girl named Lola way back then when girls had names like Rita, Eva, Mamie, Lana, Lola. This nice girl that he married worked for a cab company in Buzzards Bay, Massachusetts, and she was the dispatcher. There were two cabs in this company. The Ford. And the DeSoto. One night just before His War, Adoptadon landed in Buzzards Bay without a place to stay and called this cab company. Lola the dispatcher answered. She was such a sweet kid – bright, funny, sardonic but not cruel. The way the women were back then. The rest is history. I guess ol' Don wants us to believe there's a Lola and Corinne in every town. I guess he's right. For men like him. We'll do it and they'll take it every time. Or they'll do it and we'll leave. Or someone plays a Waylon Jennings record in the middle of the night. Or whispers rosebud. Or it was raining, you were wearing blue. Or better yet, I could have been a contender.

So Adoptadon found someplace new to call his home in Corinne's backyard for six weeks back then, which, when you think about it, is a long time to live anywhere without running water. Then something happened, as it usually does with Don: the stories differ. One story – his – had it that Corinne pressed, the way some women do, to escalate. Like move it off the ground floor up to the mezzanine. To the *premier étage* off the ol' *rez-de-chausée.* Commit thyself. Or whatever it is that women need to do. Raise high the roofbeams. Towering inferno. Who knows, but that's Don's story: Corinne needed a commitment, so he split. Out of respect for her. Natch. Every time he moves it's out of respect for the other person. For the other person's privacy. But Corinne's story – or at least the story representing an opposing point of view – is that he was already pretty sick by then and when she started to insist he see a doctor, he broke camp. There's a third story, too, and that's that Don wanted to force his son to intervene. Wanted him to step right up and volunteer. For duty. We heard he bounced around a while, moved in with a shipwright for a time, lived out at Menemsha on somebody's boat. Then he took a bad turn for the worse. And the next thing I knew Tracy's standing in the kitchen with her arms folded on her chest asking is it true. Since that could only mean one thing I answer *yep.*

'But he's dying, DC.'

'Yep.'

'Alone.'

'Well that's his choice, Trace. That's what he's chosen.'

'Since when are you the expert?'

'Since when are you?'

'Since birth.'

She fans her hands around my face like I'm some ruffled bird displaying and she makes fun of me by asking are you ready for my close-up now mister demille?

Up until the moment she died Lola thought Adoptadon was coming back. It was one of the reasons she lived her whole life in Buzzards Bay and kept her married name and kept it listed right there in the telephone book. Why don't you list it in the Yellow Pages, too, under Chump, I joked with her. She told me I knew nothing about undying love. You're carrying a torch, I said, that's turned to stone. Your arm has turned to stone. The whole affair is one big monument. Statue of liberty for christsake. And think about what *that's* inspired in the hearts of men she told me. La Mombo. Never took up with another man, never gave another one a glance as far as I know. And the cancer ate her up. She disappeared inside it. Her fingernails and toenails, I remember, were almost all of her the cancer didn't get. And her hope about Adoptadon. Up until the moment she died she was thinking of her hair, in case he walked in. Like he was going to stroll in at Massachusetts General after thirty years and say hey Lola your hair. You have about five pieces of it left. There was a little bit of time, too, right before the end, when her hope infected mine. When I wanted to believe as much as she did that here we have the kind of guy who's going to show up and help her die with both a smile and a kiss on her old lips. What a guy. Way to go ol' fella. I thought: If he only knew. I got to thinking if the old guy only knew, he'd come around. So I spent about three weeks tracing his spore. There are only so many places men like my old man could go: Towns with plenty lowlife and many visible women. Fringe towns. Harbor cities. Safe havens. Florida coast.

Our first conversation: the Mombo's dying. I am thirty.
Dondo's god-knows how old, I've never laid eyes on him: smoke
haggard voice. Eight years later smoking kills him. But
back then I ask, Do you remember a woman you were married
to some thirty years ago named Lola?

'What's it to you?'

'She's dying.'

'What's it to me? She leave me something?'

'She's got bone cancer.'

He laughs, and the laughing brings on a fit of coughing.
Who's this? he finally asks.

'Her son. She wants to see you.'

'Her son. I bet. You look like me?'

'No reason why I should.'

'Hey listen. Look. She's got my footlocker. You ever look
inside that footlocker? You should. Probably some things in
there will fit you.'

'She's at Massachusetts General. That's in Boston. She's got
about a week. She kept her married name. She likes those white
chrysanthemums.'

'Yeah.' He begins to laugh that laugh. 'Classy broad that
Lola.'

'I'll send her some from you.'

'Don't bother. Save your pennies kid.'

He's right.

She would have known the difference.

Then Tracy starts her Last Harangue.

Where women get these things: what difference does it make
the way I dress the way I eat the way I treat my father? She's
like my 'ex' was about Mombo. Mombo should have had the
State pick up her tab according to my 'ex'. Mombo shouldn't
have a semi-private room her own TV. Like Mombo shouldn't
have a real-hair wig called *la Bardot* handstitched in France

from Taiwanese adolescents hand-dipped hand-dangled hand-
dyed blond if that's what Mombo wanted. She deserved it. Shit.
Run interference between two women in my life. So Trace says,
Went to see your old man in the ward this afternoon.

Behind my back.

'Not behind your back DC. That's why I'm telling you.'

'*After* ol' el facto.'

'He came North to see you. He wants to talk to you. He's
frightened. He's old. He doesn't know how to begin. What do
you think, dignity's some kind of muscle? It's a thread. You
want to know how weak a thread it is?'

I'm not going to talk to any screaming woman about dignity
I warn her. I'm not going to talk to any screaming woman
about anything.

'I'm not screaming at you. I'm talking nice and quiet.'

Bossing me around.

It must be nice to be a self-appointed judge I tell her.

'You should know,' she says.

Like Katharine Hepburn goddam Eleanor of Aquitaine. Like
she and I aren't lovers. Like we haven't lived together on and off
the last six years. No she's going to shoot it all to hell about this
thing with Don. Until one night I end up saying Him or me.

'Fine,' she says. No contest. Into the G-chute for you, flyboy.

Women.

When I was ten years old I used to dream about his hands.
Phyllis this crone at Finley's told me I had delicate hands for a
boy my age. She grabbed my hand one day when I was paying
her for something and she said Boy what are you saving these
two hands for? You sure do have delicate hands for a big boy
your age. Like flower petals. So I used to dream about my old
man's hands. Holding mine. Or him lifting me up. The size of
bear paws, him saying These hands have saved my life more
than one time son. Being able to feel his whole strength coming

through them. His history. That storm on the North Atlantic. The avalanche on Wheeler Peak. The mountains are a kind of desert son. The big peaks. Barren. The sea's a desert too. When you've been riding her for months. He'd lost the top joint of his index finger. When an alligator jaw closed on it. So imagine my surprise to find these real small hands his index finger like his teeth stained yellow from the smoke. Plus there's nothing like the sound of some old bastard drowning in his lungs.

'Your old lady walked I hear,' he says.

'Who told you that?'

'Who else?'

'She wasn't my old lady.'

'Wanna bet?'

'I guess she took one look at you and fell in love for life, okay?'

'She's not the first.'

'Well she's the last, old man.'

That laugh of his. Like he uses it to scare ol' death away.

'So whatya wanna ask me kid? You go right ahead. Feel free. You ask me anything.'

I feel so angry I just stare.

Like everything I ever asked he ever listened.

'What'd you come here for?' I finally say.

'Well, see . . .' He tries sitting up gets all wracked up with the coughing. 'I was walkin' home one night, see? I was livin' with this woman Sadie. Sadie Tree. Like really up a Tree you get it? And she was pickin' up the bills. So for that privilege she could turn me out at one or two o'clock each night to go buy cigarettes or hand lotion or whatever the hell she thinks she needs. Ain't that the juice? Women who got money. So I'm walkin' home one night this little errand boy and I see these bums sleepin' on the beach just livin' there. On the coconuts. I musta seen them my whole life down there in the Keys you know? But never really seen them. Like you see a trillion stars your whole damn life and then one night you see them. Close. You see on over to the other side. Like California all the way from Denver, Colorado. Like for the first time I saw how really disgusting they all were. Like they didn't have a thing. Not one thing. It rained on them they just got soaking wet. They bathed themselves right in the ocean if they ever. Pissed there too. What did they care? They were nothing really. Lazy. Filthy. Bums. Freeloaders. Bastards. Couldn't even sleep inside. Couldn't even you know have a woman if they tried. If they had to. If they tried.'

I stare at him. Red-eyed. Rheumy. Each breath of his arriving like a season of bad weather.

'You ever climb mountains, go to sea?' I ask.

'Me? Never. But I slept outside. Slept outside those two whole years. It's never dark. It's always light. Don't let them tell you different. Even with cloud cover. There's always bits of light. You move inside the dark inside a room will make you squirrely. Dark's not real. You move inside they keep the windows closed you start to get real trouble with the lungs. You move inside you die. You got to keep your window open. You keep a window open do you?'

Each night. Back door, too.

'That's good. That keeps it goin'.'

She comes back in with the key she's always kept and says, 'Geeze what did you do to this place looks so different?' She doesn't have to say the old man's dead. She looks at me. 'You got a drink?'

You got amnesia I ask.

She goes to where she knows she'll find a glass of scotch and water then sits down. 'I'm going to say something, all right? I'm going to say this then that's it. There's a good chance he was crazy, DC I mean schizophrenic.'

'You dating someone Trace? I heard you've been dating.'

'So let's avoid the subject huh?'

73

'Is it Gaines the loathsome button-down? Huh? Who is it Trace? What's Gaines' last name anyway? *Burger?*'

'Look don't take his dying out on me.'

'Didn't take you long.'

'I can't believe you painted *white dots* on the ceiling.'

'Stars. They're stars. I painted white stars on the ceiling.'

'You've been drinking.'

Well smoking this shit actually.

'And Bumpy says you haven't been to work.'

For seven days.

'Come on get dressed I'll take you out.'

You'll take me out?

'I'll buy you dinner.'

You'll buy me dinner?

'And then you'll send me out for cigarettes too huh?'

'DC what are you talking about?'

Bossing me around.

He thought this was the funniest goddam joke, you want to hear it Trace? He thought this took the prize. You listening? Okay. What's the difference between a woman and a coconut? Trace? Huh? What's the difference?

She looks at me.

'Picture this: He's shouting at me at the top of his two putrid lungs. His goddam coughing. Blood. He shouts, What's the difference between a woman and a coconut? Huh? Like it's some kind of *joke*. Ol' girl? Between the woman and a coconut? I'll tell you . . .'

That bastard and his punch line:

'. . . Milk.'

Gandy Dancing

I

He wouldn't discount destiny – he'd buy the argument that someone's name could be a destination. His was.

Not his real name – his real name was a pleasant one, a good one, a non-commital, unhysteric, five-letter-long single-syllabic word which imparted nothing in particular. That's to say, it left to the imagination everything that in his own good judgment he preferred to think he was.

His name – the real one – described no notable geography. It was a name the way *land* is a name – plain and expansive, non-specific, until one uses it to differentiate it from *sky*. His was a name that differentiated him from Bobs and Freds and Mikes. It had no special ring. It had never thrilled a woman's soul, of that much he was certain. It was run-of-the-mill. But then,

77

during his last year at college a suitable moniker flitted his way.
He was walking to his car from a party one night, when
someone called to a stranger behind him, 'Hey, Kim, comin'
with us?' and Kim answered, 'Naw, I'll ride with this guy *red
car*, if it's OK with him.'

Well, yes, it was.

It was just fine.

It was filled with intrigue.

Redcar.

Vroom vroom.

Which is why he got married: He owed her a lot. Not the girl
who invented his name. Not her. He'd never seen her after that
night. Which was fitting, he felt; or, perhaps, preordained.
Certain people are destined to serve certain functions in life, he
believed. Like the seer in 'Julius Caesar'. There are seers about,
all around, he believed. People inveighing in actions against the
mundane, the consistent, the placid. Take-over people. People
who know, who decide, who decree, who invent names, mostly
women, whom you marry much less out of love than as a result
of the physical dictum of downhill momentum. Terry was one.
He married Terry because he was stalled. He needed a push,
and she was a pusher. A sweetheart, sure: but more than that,
she had a way of getting things done, making changes, keeping
a flame. They had children, thanks to Terry, two daughters.
They had the house and the car. Not a red car this time, a
taupe-colored one. Terry had opted for taupe. Not a two-seater,
either. A wagon. Full-sized. One that drove by itself and was
trying to suffocate him, Redcar believed. 'If you don't like the
car, let's trade it in,' Terry consoled him. She *was* a sweetheart. 'Why didn't you say something sooner, honey?' she
asked. 'What is it about it you don't like? Is it the color?'
He didn't know. It was a feeling, he tried to explain. A
feeling conveyed by that car that he was a cipher, a dodo, a

nothing, a cobweb, a shade. 'I understand,' Terry told him sincerely.

Shortly thereafter, their house disappeared.

Not 'disappeared' in the usual sense. What happened was one night Redcar walked home from the train and his house wasn't there. There was a house there, sure, on the lot where his house used to be, but it wasn't his. This house, wherever it came from, looked churlish. In the blue evening light, it shrank back, like a cur. 'Whose house is this?' he asked Terry. 'Whose do you think?' she asked back. It looked the same, sort of the same as it always had looked, once he was inside. The furniture looked much the same. Then things started to happen. The paint peeled. Window panes rooted fissures. Seismographic traces surfaced through plaster. He was unprepared for this kind of behavior in a house. It was an insult. 'A man's house ought to be his best friend,' he said to Terry. 'His castle,' she told him. But Redcar felt his house around him the way a stallion responds to a stall. In his heart, he paced. He no longer slept the sleep he had known. He ceased to dream. He felt that if he dreamed the rafters could corral his visions, the floorboards would rise up and make a coffin for each one. He didn't dream. He didn't linger over color photographs of mountains in the glossies. He didn't nod at intrigue in the fiction that he read. He didn't notice steamy fragrance rising from the sidewalk vendors in the rain, until one day in December he stepped down off the commuter train onto the platform in Grand Central Station and smelled something. He stood there, incapable of moving, as if blinded by a photo flash or captioned in a paragraph on paper. This thing, whatever it was, this trip line to his senses, this depth charge buried in his reason, had gone off before, one night at the opera when he sat down at a performance of 'Aida' that Terry had dragged him to and found himself sitting beside a beautiful woman, who, when he dared to look more closely at her, was the most perfect creature he had almost ever put his hand next to. He longed to brush his arm against her, it was as if his skin and bones were metal in the presence of a magnet, but he couldn't. He couldn't act. He held his longing down and kept it hidden until one day he walked into a department store on Fifth Avenue during his lunch hour and tried to see if he could locate her perfume among the tester bottles displayed on trays along glass counters. This seemed a quest a hundred times less likely to be satisfied that those of the Knights Templars or the Argonauts, and he was emboldened by its affect of unreality until, that is, he found it. He found *her*, inside a perfume bottle. And finding *her* proved beyond a doubt that she was waiting to be found. Which argued for adventure and discovery and asked a question of his will. Which upset his acquired sense of balance terribly. And now, after an interlude of several years, this thing was happening again. He smelled *train*. He smelled the smell of track and he smelled metal. He smelled fuel. He smelled distance, he smelled long odds. He smelled blues.

When it was over, he dusted himself off.

He walked upstairs to the Concourse in Grand Central Station and proceeded, as he always did, past the broker's kiosk, past the off-track betting windows, past his many fellow men on their ways to work in New York City. Three hours later he was thinking it all through, eating nachos at a stand-up counter, talking to a man in snakeskin shoes in the airport in the city of Atlanta.

It was the woman's fault, he would tell Terry, if he called her. It was the woman who sold tickets in Grand Central Station who impelled him into doing what he had to do. It was she who set the plan in motion, laid the route out, wrote up his itinerary. It was simple, really. He would travel out to California, turn around and come right back. See the country, the whole sweep of it at once, by train, and be back home before the kids and Terry would have time to notice. The trip would take eight days. Which wasn't much, when you stop to think about it.

'Is tha' righ'?' the man in snakeskin shoes was moved to ask him.

'It'll take me even less time,' Redcar said, 'because I'll catch up with the train leaving New Orleans. That'll save me three days' travel time right there.'

'Is tha' righ'?'

'I missed *The Sunset Crescent* when it left New York three days ago. *The Sunset Crescent* is the train that goes along the whole East Coast into Louisiana. You see, three days ago I didn't even know I was going to take this trip.'

'Is tha' righ'?'

'I just decided it this morning. See the whole darn country. See the whole darn place. I've never seen the West before, except in movies. I've never even seen the Mississippi. You want to know what else? I've never seen a man in snakeskin shoes before.'

'They's lizard, son.'

'No kidding?'

'Gila monsters. Two per shoe. That's four, all total. You ain't one of those Eastern lizard lovers, are you?'

'Lizard lovers?'

'Righ'.'

'No, sir.'

'Tha's good.'

'What's a lizard lover?'

'Put it this way: when you're a lizard lover, you love lizards.'

The man reached into his jacket pocket and took a billfold out and gave Redcar his business card. It said he was a zipper manufacturer from Wheeling, West Virgina, and he bought Redcar a beer and told him Velcro was about to do his business in. The man made zippers out to be a long sad story and Redcar was relieved when the man's flight was called. There were a lot of military passing through the airport, Redcar noticed. Young men on their way back home for Christmas. When one of them sat down beside him with his Army duffle bag packed to its

81

capacity, Redcar suddenly remembered he was traveling with nothing but a rumpled overcoat and a rolled up copy of *The Wall Street Journal*. He ought to have a toothbrush, he considered. And an extra pair of socks. The only times he'd gone away on a vacation previous to this, he'd gone with Terry and they shared a suitcase which Terry always packed. A pair of sunglasses, he thought, might come in handy, too. For arriving in New Orleans. For traveling through Texas. Through the desert. On to California.

Redcar's thoughts were interrupted when his flight was called and as he sauntered down the boarding ramp he felt his heart grow lighter. He tried to catch the eyes of several passengers he passed, to signal his excitement, but everybody failed to give him notice. The stewardess seemed blasé when she greeted him. He wanted to leap about and announce to everyone that he was setting out to go across the country, the whole United States, an entire continent, and back, by train. But no one seemed at all inspired by the prospect of their journey, or his, either. They didn't seem like travelers at all, more like people waiting on a line to purchase something plain and fundamental like a roll of baling twine.

His seat was by a window in a row of three, and when he reached it an old lady was already settled in the aisle seat with her cane across her lap. Redcar had to help to lift her out, then help to lift her in again. 'I hope nobody comes,' he said, referring to the empty seat between them.

'*What?*' she snapped. She touched the knob end of her cane behind her ear.

'I said, I hope another person doesn't come along,' Redcar said again, nodding toward the empty seat.

'*I* had hoped *you* wouldn't,' she informed him.

When they took off, her cane fell to the floor and rolled against his feet. She asked him if he'd hand her back her 'walking stick'. He could hear the South all through her accent. 'Are you visitin' your people?' she asked.

'No, I'm off on an adventure, m'am.'

'*Don't give me that!* What's your name?' she snapped.

'It's Redcar, m'am.'

'Redcar what?'

'Plain "Redcar", m'am.'

'*Don't try and give me that one, either!*'

Redcar hated when a woman yelled at him, so he started to look out the window. Soon the pines and clay gave way to inlets etched like Aztec pictographs, then the plane descended over Lake Pontchartrain and landed on a runway watched by several dozen snowy egrets and Redcar passed through his first time zone. By one-thirty local time he was sitting in the front seat of a taxicab, his tie and vest and suit jacket discarded, talking to the driver, on his way to Union Station on Loyola Avenue, New Orleans. 'Take me to the River first,' he said.

'What you want with that ol' river?' he was asked.

'Want to see it.'

'You ain't never seen that nasty river?'

'Never.'

'Man! I seen that river every day since I was born.'

'I bet it's something, huh?'

'It's nuffin', man. She the nuffin'est bad news a man can gets.'

They went to Jackson Square and Redcar walked up the embankment and then before him was the Mississippi River. He watched a river barge moving what appeared to be a cargo of black sand downriver toward the Gulf. Suddenly he felt an altered sense of gravity. He felt lighter than the river. He felt certain if he dived in her that he would rise and float, that the center of his gravity was braided in her current. This unexpected pleasure, this lightening, was something like a regained territory he had one time occupied. It was everything that he could do to keep from taking off his shoes and dancing to the far side with her.

At Union Station Redcar bought a toothbrush, toothpaste, razor, a copy of the local *Times-Picayune*, two t-shirts for his daughters that said 'Louisiana World Exposition' and one that said 'Cajun Country' in big letters under a picture of a snarling alligator, for himself. He walked into the train yard and walked the full length of the train along the platform, looking over all the cars. They were enormous and mysterious as unassembled brontosaurus bones. Coupled, they completed a behemoth. The train was big enough to be a rolling city. It seemed to generate a climate. Noise was churning from it, even as it waited, standing still. A trainman was inspecting every car, checking facts against a list held to a clipboard. Redcar walked beside him for a while in silence. 'How come there are two engines?' Redcar finally asked.

'Big train,' he was told.

'Are you the boss around here?' Redcar asked.

'The train's the boss, I'm just the fireman.'

'You mean in case there's fire?'

The trainman shook his head. 'It used to mean I *made* the fire. Now that everything's electric, we kept the name. You know, "fire man". Our whole job these days is pretty much just checking out the road at redblocks.'

'*Redblocks?*'

'Yep.'

'What's a redblock?'

'A red signal on the track. Indicatin' trouble. It's computerized these days. Problem is, the damn computer can't tell the difference between ice on the track and a real rockslide. I'm the one who gets to go ahead and check it.'

'You go out alone?'

'Yes, sir.'

'Like a scout?'

'I reckon.'

'If we get a redblock on this trip, could you take me with you when you check the track?'

'Well, like I said, it doesn't happen often. Don't get the wrong opinion. We keep to schedule nine times out of ten.'

'I don't care about your schedule,' Redcar said.

The trainman touched his cap.

'How far you ridin' with us?' he asked Redcar.

'To L.A.'

'Los Angeles. Okay. I'll find you.'

'I'm in Coach.'

'I know how to find you.'

'Name's Redcar.'

The fireman looked sad. 'Well, that's some name, now, isn't it?' he mourned. 'Like a caboose.'

Redcar had hoped someone was going to holler, '*All aboard!*', but the train lurched slightly, huffed, and then began to move by inches out of Union Station. He rode in the doorway where he could feel the wind and smell the track and sense the movement, then the Chief of On-Board Services told him to sit down because the tickets needed to be taken. The coach was crowded, full of noise, and it wasn't 'til the train was crossing the Huey Long Bridge over the Mississippi with New Orleans in the distance that Redcar thought he ought to plan a time and place where he could make a call to Terry. He consulted a train schedule and read there was a stop in Houston at eleven. New York time was one hour behind and since he often stayed at work real late, it wouldn't seem too strange to call that late to say he wasn't coming home for dinner because he was in Houston, Texas, on his way by train to California. No doubt she'd understand. In the meantime, the Chief of On-Board Services came by for his ticket. 'I'll be giving a talk soon on the address system about the discovery of Tabasco sauce,' the Chief advised him. This pleased Redcar. It pleased him that Tabasco sauce could be discovered, like crude oil or another planet. The idea of it made him feel like being silly, sharing a good laugh. But when he looked around, there wasn't anyone who looked as though she'd understand.

The train was running parallel to bayous and passed a group of houses with children playing in the yard with goats tied up where rusty water tanks were banked against the shabby clapboard sidings. It passed a cemetery where the dead were laid above ground, owing to the swampy land. The rows of white crypts looked like rows of beds. The train passed a delivery truck, the kind one sees up North dispensing ice cream, painted with the slogan, 'SHRIMP. WE HONNER FOOD STAMPS.' Every now and then it passed a kid who stood and waved. After a while Redcar decided it was time to stretch his legs. He got up. He walked as far as he could walk forward, through the cars, then he turned around and walked as far as he could walk, the other way. He ended in the lounge behind a Bloody Mary.

He got out at every station.

He got out at New Iberia, Louisiana, where Tabasco sauce is made; and at Lafayette, where Cajuns live; and at Lake Charles, where there isn't anything. At New Iberia the conductor had cautioned him, 'You don't want to get off here, sir,' and again at Lafayette the conductor said, 'There's no time for you to leave the train at this-here station.' But by the time they pulled into Lake Charles, the conductor had gotten used to Redcar's way of jumping from the train to go to see deserted stations. After Lake Charles, they crossed the Sabine River from Louisiana into Texas and the silvery flat landscape of the rice fields darkened with oil derricks, and Redcar went up to the dining car for dinner. He sat with a man and a woman on their way to Phoenix, Arizona. They had their six-year old son with them, who kept making pills from strips of paper napkin and eating them. The woman showed Redcar photographs of an adolescent girl. 'I'm talkin' to this man about your sister,' she told the little boy. 'Tell this man your sister's name.'

'I don't know it.'

'You don't know your sister's name?' the father asked.

'I forgot it.'

'You forgot your sister's name?' the mother said.

The boy looked out the window. 'I didn't bring it with me. I didn't pack it in my suitcase. It's not with me on this train,' he said.

Houston was the first big stop along the route and Redcar was looking forward to it. A city, he expected, was a place where people lived and worked, a place much like the inside of a turbine, where one could feel an endless humming. But Houston felt more like the inside of a stone. It was dark and hot and still and humid. 'Five minutes, sir,' the conductor told him, when he got off the train. 'We don't want to lose you.'

The Houston station was a new one – boxy, well-lit, painted a light green, furnished with five rows of pews. The space could be as much a transit depot as a place of worship, Redcar thought, and when he looked at the expressions on the people's faces he was certain it was being used as both. Joylessness strayed through this station, trailing someone's tattered wrap. Redcar came in one door, walked through, walked straight out the other. He felt lost and in a panic. The city, Houston, gloamed on the perimeter like steam above a stone. There were garlands of bright green and garish crimson tinsel strung up on the station's walls. When he'd come in through the doors everyone had turned to him, expectantly. It was the feeling that they looked on him as if he were a cold dart shot into their steaming heart that kept him going through the chamber. So he never did call Terry. He sat up all night, through the Texas landscape, through San Antonio, wondering where so many trains were coming from, that kept on coming, blowing their sad horns so frequently and at such great distance to warn that they were crossing. In the middle of the night he realized those train horns were coming from the engine up ahead, his engine, and that like the train, itself, he was trailing on a sound, its sound, in passing.

II

The day dawned west of Del Rio, Texas, where Redcar watched it from a window in the lounge car. They were moving over desert range now, stubbly, unremarkable land east of the Pecos River, where the surface of the stone was just beneath the dusty topsoil. The skeletal gantries of the windmills seemed born of the same botany as the beavertail, the sage, the mesquite and the cactus. Pink shale and yellow schist ebbed and flowed under the cattle. There was little sign of human habitation anywhere. When the train stopped at Sanderson, Texas, Redcar stepped out into sub-freezing weather and a scape of human temporariness unlike anything he'd ever known. Everything was made of rusted tin and weathered lumber. Sand had blasted colors to a same blanched, bony yellow. The roads, if paved, were drifted over with debris and yellow dust. 'Retirement Village, huh?' the Chief joked with him, as they flapped their arms against the cold. Redcar murmured, 'Jesus Christ.'

'Yo're in Texas now, boy!'

'I guess the hell I am . . .'

The fireman came toward him and asked, 'Hey, Mister Redcar, what do you think of this-here town?'

'Keep it.'

'Devil said that, too, I reckon. You'll like Alpine, though. Alpine's comin' up next, about two hundred miles. Got architecture. Are you lookin' into architecture, Mister Redcar? What you lookin' into?'

'Architecture sounds like it will do.'

'Well, you'll like Alpine, then. New Mexico's a pretty state. Don't come no prettier. Get lucky, we can take ourselves a pretty walk behind El Paso. Sometimes we get a bit of trouble on the road 'tween there and Deming. A redblock.'

'I'm looking forward to it,' Redcar said. As if it were a destination.

They hit El Paso twenty minutes in advance of schedule, so Redcar had a chance to stroll the town. He walked down to the bus depot and around the new civic center. In a burned out lot near the bridge across the Rio Grande a dozen men of different ages stood around and shrugged against the cold and drank from bottles wrapped in paper bags. Redcar stopped to watch them. When they noticed him they turned away. Finally someone hurled an empty bottle at him. Redcar almost made a call to Terry, but when he got back to the station there was no time 'cause the train was pulling out.

He dined that night on catfish, featured on the menu as 'Catch of the Day'.

Near sunset Redcar saw a herd of antelope.

In Tucson, Arizona, very late at night, he got off the train and roamed the streets around the Toole Street Station. He had learned that cities turn their backs on railroad stations. On the streets adjacent this one there were the Hotel Congress, four liquor stores, the Jackpot Arcade & Bingo Parlor, a thrift store and the Arizona State Unemployment Office. He found a Catholic church built in the Spanish Mission style ten blocks from the station. Next to it there was an orange tree, the first one Redcar had ever seen. It was half the size of his yard back home and gravid with its fruit. Beneath the tree there was a statue of the infant Jesus in His crèche flanked by His parents and the shepherds and the wisemen and the sheep and donkeys and the camels, lighted by two yellow spotlights which made the oranges on the orange tree glow in Technicolor. It was hard to think of them as things that could be eaten, touched, picked: stolen. He confessed this to the Chief when they were sitting in the lounge car after midnight that same night, looking out at the black desert before Phoenix, and the Chief said, 'I suppose you have to be a Catholic to appreciate it.'

'I'm not Catholic,' Redcar argued.

'Neither were those oranges, son.'

'What would you have done?'

'Not stolen any, same as you.'

'Because it is a sin?'

'Hell, no!'

'Why not, then?'

'Because I hate the taste of oranges. Always have. Ever since the Navy. Lemons, too. They just don't seem to mix with salt-sea air. How 'bout you?' the Chief asked. Redcar stared at him. 'How 'bout me what?' He took a sip of bourbon. 'Been in the Navy?' he was asked.

He'd been traveling for two days and two nights without sleep when he stepped down from the train in California the next morning and felt strange, as if he'd shifted back in time into the 40's, to the time when he was born. The feeling came to him from something in the air. It was the train station, he realized, the way it looked, the way it felt: it seemed to have enclosed the time in which it had been built and kept it there, if time were such a thing that could be kept that way, by spaces, and held prisoner. 'You lost, Mister Redcar?' someone asked him. It was the fireman. 'This is some place, ain't it?' he marveled. 'You won't beat this place for architecture. You an architect or something, Mister Redcar?' 'Something,' Redcar answered. They walked through Union Station to the entrance near the parking lot on North Alameda where the fireman's wife was waiting for him, driving an old Buick. 'Somebody meeting you here, are they?' the fireman asked.

'No,' Redcar answered.

'Give you a lift somewheres, then?'

'No, thanks, this is as far as I'm going.'

The fireman kissed his wife, then Redcar watched them drive

away. He imagined a whole life for them – not as a series of events, but as a structure seen, a union of notched timbers, a life expounded in split rails. He went across North Alameda against the light and got caught up in the traffic between disused trolley tracks. He hadn't expected to find trolley tracks in tinsel town – the tracks ran, burnished like a lode or like two lightning rods toward the reaches of the city. Nothing ran along them anymore, neither lightning bolts nor any hope of payoff. Redcar stood between them in the middle of the avenue for what seemed a long time, staring at the optical illusion of a point, from his perspective, where the parallels would join. He knew that if he took a step along the tracks in either one of two directions the point at which the tracks appeared to meet would slip away, would slide back equal distance to his forward motion, so he stood quite still, checking the illusion, keeping it in sight until the sun rose high and the light collecting on the tracks obliterated distance with mirage. He thought, 'I'm in California.'

He tried to understand it was as far as he could go.

III

The Eastbound *Desert Wind* departed Union Station, Los Angeles, that afternoon, the sixth day before Christmas, packed to its capacity with a mob intent for Vegas. They were drinkers and card players – randy, loud and deep into their booze by the time the train left San Bernardino. They played for nickels and for quarters but they played intently, ploddingly and hard, like oxen. They filled the coach and lounge cars with a sense of sullen restlessness, waiting for that thing to happen, that number to come up, that winning card to show. 'You want in?' a woman asked him as he lingered near a game of blackjack in the lounge car.

'I'm just watching,' Redcar said.

The woman, chewing gum and smoking a brown cigarette, smiled. 'Let me ask you somethin'. We're takin' a straw poll here. What would you say God's first name was?'

'Oscar,' Redcar said.

'"Oscar God", that doesn't stand too bad,' she said. 'You want to put some money on it?'

'No, thanks,' Redcar said.

'Not a gambler?'

'No, m'am,' Redcar said.

'You got good sense. I like a man who knows when he's a loser. You lost. God's name is Rosemary,' she said.

Las Vegas rose like a brilliant movie set out of the desert and the train rolled right into the Union Plaza Hotel where passengers disembarked under ornate chandeliers onto a red carpet on a platform lined with one-arm bandits. More than half the people on the train got off at Vegas. As she watched them leave the new Chief of On-Board Services murmured, 'Go to hell.' Her name was Jeannie. She was a big woman, buxom, and she liked to rub her hands together as she spoke, as if forming little pies. Redcar asked her if she would ask the new fireman if he could tag along if there were any redblocks. Jeannie pressed her hands together and answered, 'That depends.'

'On what?'

'On the fireman.'

'Well, could you ask him?'

'Maybe,' she said. To the look that Redcar gave her, she commented, 'He's a doozie, honey.'

It was dark when they arrived in Salt Lake City, at six-fifteen the next morning. Snow had fallen in the night. One of the passengers Redcar talked to outside Caliente, Nevada, wagered that Union Pacific Station in Salt Lake City was the most impressive railroad station in the West, so Redcar hauled himself into the cold to go to see it. It was like a court room. There were murals painted into arches all around the barrel-vaulted ceiling. *If you're going to pass through here*, the mural seemed to say, *this place is going to teach you something.* Redcar wondered what that something was, what lesson he was meant to draw from men depicted bearing arms and driving teams of oxen pulling Conestoga wagons: men and clergymen depicted reverent and genuflecting before a locomotive engine stoked and headstrong with a furnace fed and fiery with coal. He walked outside to see if it were true of Salt Lake City, as it had been true of Houston, San Antonio, Tucson and Phoenix, that the city faced away from its own railroad station. In the freezing predawn dark at the front of Union Pacific Station, some taxicabs were parked. Drivers were standing 'round, drinking steaming coffee from their paper cups, talking in that flat, extracted Utah accent that chips the English syllables away from one another like a pick-axe making bits of stone-faced mountain fly. 'Flinty' was the word that he was looking for: flinty men, flinty mountain, flinty hearts. Unlike the cities in the Southwest, Salt Lake faced her railroad tracks, he saw. The city started here. Its heart was up a broad street seven blocks away, but there was nothing to obstruct the view from here to what had to be the natural outcome of the settlers' flintiness: a spark. The spark of mysticism. The Mormon Tabernacle.

'For godsake,' Redcar said, when he saw it.

'*Exactly,*' someone chided him.

'Don't it look just like the Wizard's place in "The Wizard of Oz"?' Jeannie asked him when he came back to the train and told her where he'd been. 'You get off at every stop?' she asked, while assessing his growth of beard and the smoky circles 'round his eyes, the way that women do. 'That's the kid's dream, isn't it?' she asked, making little pancakes with her palms.

'What is?'

'To get out at every station,' she reminded him.

'Is it?'

'Sure.'

She blew into her hands.

'And not have any thoughts about tomorrow.'

'Like Peter Pan, you mean?' Redcar asked her, rising to the challenge.

'Not like Peter Pan,' she pointed out. 'He *flew*.' She wasn't joking.

The whole next day the Rockies kept him in their thrall. To him they seemed to be expression of the sheer exasperation of the earth's crust with its gravity. *One* more try! he almost heard the highest of them shouting, having pushed its own weight up its slope to its own peak and there to have to end. Some of them made temples of themselves – great, grave, graceful parthenons – while others turned to mausoleums or dressed their somber stones as pyramids. *Human beings crossed these*, is the single most recurring thought: and then its corollary: *Why?* What form would an emotion have to take that could compel a man to try his fate on this geography? Why not stay somewhere nice and flat like Kansas or Nebraska? 'I bet these mountains look a whole lot different in the summer,' a young woman across the aisle from him in the lounge car baited an old cowboy sitting in a window seat.

'Nope,' he answered.

'You mean they don't look any different in the spring or summer?'

'Yep.'

'Not even in the spring?'

The cowboy looked away.

'That's hard to believe,' the young woman said.

She looked at him expectantly.

He couldn't see a foothold in her line of talk for making conversation, so he didn't.

Redcar wondered which of them regretted it.

*

He was sound asleep when Jeannie touched him on the shoulder, and he jolted. It was pitch dark on the windows. It was very quiet. The train was standing still.

They descended from the train, Redcar first, jumping down into a foot of powder snow over a sheer embankment. He fell to his knees, sliding five or six feet in the snow before recovering. Jeannie cursed him. She sat down in the car door and hung her feet over the side. He climbed back up the hill. 'Here,' she said. She pulled her rubber boots off. 'You can't go hiking over half of Colorado in a pair of penny loafers,' she said. Redcar hoisted himself back into the car and traded his wet loafers for her boots. 'They're still warm,' he mentioned. 'We try our best,' she joked. He let himself down onto the track again. 'You better hurry,' Jeannie said. She rubbed her stockinged feet together. 'That's him, up there,' she told him. She shone her light along the line of cars toward the engines, silhouetting a lone figure in the distance who signalled back. Then, even as they watched him, he turned and started down the track. 'Get a move on,' Jeannie said. 'Here – take my torch.' She handed him her flashlight and he started out, about eight car-lengths behind the unknown fireman. Beside him, on his right, the huge body of the train bridled and thrummed dissatisfaction. On his left, the ground banked steeply for a few feet down a gully then climbed gently up snow covered foothills of dark pines. Ahead of him the shadows on the low, snowy hills lay etched in the penumbra of the engine car's bright headlight. He could make out where the track must lay beneath the snow, because it cut a narrow swath between the rocks and hills. Along the center of this path, several hundred yards ahead of him, he could see the outline of the gantry and the single red light of the redblock that had stopped them.

As he passed the engines, the train's roar fell away behind him. He could hear his footsteps in the snow, he could see the fireman's black tracks between the rails. He turned Jeannie's flashlight off and walked within the bright light of the engine's beacon, conscious of its power on his back. Ahead of him the track curved slightly to the left, turning from the train's light toward the contours of the night. Just beyond this, where the track fell into shadow, the fireman stopped and waited for him, as if the intersection of shadow with light was a juncture, same as any street corner. When Redcar came up to him, the fireman struck a match and lit a cigarette and Redcar got a good, brief, flickery impression of his face. He was a small-featured man with quick dark eyes. He was half a head shorter than Redcar, thin and wiry. 'Thayer,' he announced. He said it in a voice that sounded older than he looked.

'Redcar,' Redcar told him.

Thayer let him have a nod. 'You look like you're a Redcar,' he acknowledged. 'On vacation?'

'Well, I . . .'

'High-school mechanics teacher from Mason City, Iowa, someplace like that?'

Redcar felt the man lining up his sights on him, so he said, 'I smelled train four days ago and got on one out of New Orleans.'

Thayer rubbed his hand across his beard. 'Good woman, New Orleans,' he stated. He looked down the track toward the redblock and smoked. 'What's your motive in this?' he asked.

'I don't know.'

'Don't know?'

Thayer looked at him.

'No clue whatsoever?'

'None.'

Thayer smiled.

'You follow beautiful women around in the street, too, do you?'

'Not lately.'

Thayer pinched his cigarette between his thumb and fore-finger and pulled a deep long gift from it.

'Why not, boy?' he prodded.

Redcar stared at him, a little uncomfortable, not knowing what to say. Thayer leaned toward him, inviting a confidence, and Redcar bent his head down to hear what the older man had to say.

'See,' Thayer said, confidentially, 'the only good answer to that is that you married one.' He looked at Redcar, expectantly. 'Did you marry one?'

Redcar nodded.

'Lucky man!' Thayer told him. 'How many times?'

'Once,' Redcar admitted.

'Lucky man!' Thayer shone his flashlight down the track and tricked it slowly, left then right, letting the light swing like a pendulum. 'Everybody ought to marry.' He focused the torch beam on the signal up ahead, then added, '*Once.*'

They started walking toward the redblock, and Redcar felt the night move in. It moved as weather moves, shifting its mass. The sky got wider, closer – Redcar felt like he was diving toward it. Thayer cupped his palm over the torch beam, so that nothing broke the expanse of hills under the night, except the sound of their walking. When they reached the signal, Thayer focused a light on the switchblock, kicked the rail and murmured, 'Ice.' The short-wave radio in his coat pocket crackled. He looked at Redcar. 'Half a mile to the next signalblock. I've got to keep on checking 'til I come up against a light that's green. You comin' with me?'

'You bet.'

Thayer spoke into the short-wave, and they started off. They were trekking up a slow grade, Redcar feeling the incline in his chest. The night was clear, the stars sharp; there was no moon. Slowly Redcar became aware of the infinite futility of movement. So he stopped. The earth was tilting toward its apogee in its orbit 'round the sun; the morning star was rising somewhere over the Pacific, so he stopped. He turned around and looked back down the gentle hillside at the silent body of the train stretched like a coded message strung behind him on a line. He started to breathe with difficulty, drinking sips of cold air at the crystal lip of night like someone nearly dead of thirst falling on the edge of an oasis. Thayer came up beside him and struck a match and lit another cigarette.

'The *loco*-motive, son,' he pointed out.

They walked again, while Thayer smoked, and in a while Redcar could see the next signalblock through the pine trees, in the distance, shining green. He knew Thayer had seen it first, by the way he threw his cigarette down on the track. The lawbook stated every foot of track had to be secured by a fireman's on-sight inspection between switchblocks when one was red, so they traipsed all the way to the green light and Thayer radioed the brakeman on the short-wave, then they started back.

'I saw an elk here a couple years ago,' Thayer mentioned. 'Came out of the trees down there and walked right up the track. Scared the living pants right off me.'

'You mean you saw the elk right here?'

'Uh-huh.'

'How can you tell this is the place?'

Thayer trained his flashlight on a rock formation just above them and said, 'Notch.' Then he arced the beam across the tracks to a single white-barked tree among the pines and noted, 'Birch.' Then he ran the torch beam in a straight line up the track to the nearest timber and said, 'Pole.' He highlighted these three points again in quick succession, and where the mid-points of the lines drawn between them intersected the railroad track, he said, '*Elk*.' He said, 'Son, I *live* these tracks.' He extinguished the torch and he and Redcar stood in the absolute silence while he lit himself another cigarette. 'I'll tell you how bad it gets,' he said. 'I got up to Boston last year, see, because my kid decides he's going to marry this nice Boston girl in a church wedding. So I go to the church wedding, all right? And I go to the reception, are you with me? And then, I don't remember how this happened, see, but then the next thing I remember is I'm climbing over the turnstile in a 'T' station in the middle of the night, across from my hotel, so I can get down on the track. Do you understand what I'm saying?' Thayer looked at Redcar in the darkness, but Redcar was afraid to break the spell. 'And it was *beautiful!*' Thayer continued. 'Do you know what I'm talking about when I say it was *beautiful?* Quiet as a church, boy. Miles and miles. Then after a while the tracks come up aboveground and I find myself down around these old deserted buildings there in Boston Harbor just around the dawn. And I spend all day there. Walking around, just sitting there. In my tuxedo. And my kid yells at me, "Dad! Where the hell have you been?" and I tell him, "Son, I just spent one of the finest days of my life," and he says, "Oh? Really? Where did you go?" and I say, "I walked the subway tracks and looked at old deserted buildings." And I see this look, you know that *look* they get and I say to myself, the hell with it, I'm going to tell this to him and if he gets it, he gets it, and if he doesn't the hell with them all, so I say, "And, son, do you know *why* I like to look at old deserted buildings?" and he says, "No, dad," and I say, "Because they're *lovely* and they're *falling down*. And because *I'm* lovely. And *I'm* falling down." . . .'

Redcar held his breath and stood very still for what seemed a long time. Then he noticed that Thayer had turned his torch light back on and was playing it across the sky.

'They're up there, you know,' Thayer confided.

'What?' Redcar said, hoping this was a joke.

'I know you're up there!' Thayer shouted to the night, swinging the torch light through the stars. He ran forward, hopping around, throwing his arms out, hooting: 'I know you're out there, all right! Don't think you can get away without me! Hey!' He dropped the torch and started to throw snow with both hands, running back and forth, jumping up and down: 'I'm yelling at you! Hey! What about it! Hey! What about John Thayer?! Hey! Don't forget about me –!'

He tossed one last snowball to the sky, picked up his

flashlight and came toward Redcar. Redcar's heart was in his mouth. 'What the *hell* –?' he started.

Thayer lit a cigarette and trained his torch light down the center of the railroad track. He shrugged.

'*Gandy dancing,*' he proposed.

IV

The wind in Iowa, coming from wherever wind comes from as it builds across the plains, accumulates such force across so great a flat expanse, that it whips up rills of snow as high as houses against corn silos; then comes Illinois, like a compression, and one begins to feel the East.

Coming to Chicago from the West is coming to the first big Eastern city. Chicago is *The* City. There's nothing like it west of there. There's nothing like it, anywhere.

Redcar stepped from *The Desert Wind* onto the platform at Union Station in Chicago, and he could feel the building vibrate with trains and noise and wind and people running, calling to each other. Men dressed as Santa Clauses, ringing bells, mingled in with Redcaps pushing luggage carts and travelers carrying shopping bags of Christmas presents. Christmas carols piped over the loudspeakers and vendors hawked cut flowers. Redcar stopped beside a fluted granite column in the main hall at a phone booth and used a credit card to place a call to Terry. He heard the phone at home ring once, and then she answered. The train station was very loud. He cupped his left hand to the receiver. 'Terry!' he shouted. 'Can you hear me, honey? It's me! Redcar! I'm in Chicago –!'

'*Who?!*' he heard her answer.

He pivoted away from the main hall, trying to shield the mouthpiece from all the noise. 'Listen! I'm going to take a cab out to the airport now –!'

'*Steve?!*' he heard her shout. '*Steve!* Is that you?! Steve, where the hell have you been?!'

'It's okay!' Redcar shouted back. 'I'm in *Chicago* –!'

He looked over his shoulder and saw Jeannie and Thayer walking through the main hall with some of the other train employees.

A dining car steward named Orsone noticed him and waved.

'The girls and I have been through *hell*!' Terry was yelling at him. 'Did you have an accident?! I thought you had been *kidnapped*! I called the FBI!'

'Hey, Mister Redcar!' Orsone called.

Thayer caught his eye.

Jeannie smiled at him.

'What do you mean you're in Chicago? What's going on? Steve? *Answer me*!'

'You ridin' with us again real soon, hey, Mister Redcar?' Orsone shouted to him.

His wife was screaming, 'Steve?! *Steve!* Are you listening to me? When can I expect you *home* –?'

Redcar put the phone down, and his answer rang the air as something like a train attaining track, just as it leaves the station.

Kafkas

IN DER NACHT SIND ALLE KATZEN GRAU, Fran reads. 'That means
IN DER NACHT – in the night – SIND ALLE – sing all – KATZEN GRAU
– cats grey, right? How's that? We're getting pretty *schlau* with
all this *deutsch-Verfasser*, huh? IN DER NACHT SIND ALLE KATZEN
GRAU. In the night, all the grey cats sing. Good. We're breezing
right along here. Grey cats. And all this time you thought they
were Comanche Indians.'

She arranges what she'll need tonight before her on the
kitchen table, near the phone: her pen, the logbook and the
map. She'll be working towns in the far Southeastern region,
Miami Beach, Fort Lauderdale, Key Biscayne, Coral Gables
. . . Orlando? No, no. Too *katholisch*, too *christlich*, she decides.

She hears the sounds of Sherm's and Dina's lovemaking
subside in their room. Soon they'll be fast asleep; Sherm, almost
immediately. Dina in a little while. Then she can begin to make

105

her calls. Sometimes Dina gets up and goes into the bathroom afterward, depending on the time of month. Sometimes she comes into the kitchen for a glass of water. Fran tries to ignore their sounds. Who wants to listen to her sister's lovemaking? Especially, who wants to hear Sherman shout about it? They could be a little quieter, that's all. Like they used to be. Is it possible they weren't making love the first month after she moved in? Maybe her staying here is good for them. Maybe her presence in the guest room gets their love life going. Sure, try that on for size. She's beginning to pick up on some resentment coming from Sherman about her being around, so maybe she'll remind him how his sex life has picked up, since she's moved in, that's what she'll do. And if Dina comes out now for a glass of water, she'll just sit here like she's working on her resumé. Nobody needs to know she's calling Kafkas.

'Operator?' she starts off, after a few minutes. 'Yes, in the Miami Beach vicinity. *Kafka*, kay-ay-eff, kay-ay. What? No, kay-ay-*eff*. *Eff* as in *Frohlichkeit*. That's right. What? No, I'm sorry, I don't have a first name, just read me what you've got. Just read the misters. I'm only interested in misters. No mizzes, no misters-and-missuses, no children's telephones. Just misters. What? I'm sorry, darling, no. I don't have his address. You have *what*? You have *how many*? Thirteen? Darling, you've just made my week. I think you've struck a gold mine here, the famous ol' *Topf* of *Gold*, as you might say. Why don't you read them to me and I'll jot them down . . uh huh . . . uh huh . . . uh huh. Well, thank *you*. You mean we have a choice? I thought we *had* to dial ay-tee and tee . . .'

A night of thirteen Kafkas! This is the most she's ever had! You'd have thought Manhattan and the Boroughs would be loaded with them, but she'd exhausted New York City, Yonkers, Nassau and Westchester Counties all in about two hours a couple weeks ago. Then L.A. And then Chicago. Then Baltimore and Washington. Then San Francisco. Then the entire state of Delaware. Now Southern Florida:

'Hello, Wally Kafka of Emerald Bay, Miami? Hello. This is Fran Koslow calling. Doctor Koslow, pee-aitch-dee. Wally, what I'd like to ask you is – *of course* I know what time it is.

'Hello?'

Der Maulwurf. She runs a line through Wally's name and Wally's number on her list. *Der Schwindler.* Wally. What is 'Wally' short for? *Walrus?* Sure, they're all related, all of them throwbacks to that decimated Kafka strain, but do they have to be so *unhöflich* to someone calling in the night?

'Hello?

'Vance Kafka? Vance – yours is an unusual name for a Kafka. Where are you from, Vance, if you don't mind my asking?

'Of course I know what time it is.

'Hello?'

So much for fancy Vance.

So much for Thomas, too; and Stewart, Simon, Rico –

Rico Kafka?

'Let me ask you something, if I may, Rico. Are you Czech, by any chance?'

'Am I check? Sure. I'm check bery bery good.'

He laughs.

She laughs with him.

'It's just that Rico is a Spanish-sounding name,' she says.

'Spanish, *sí*!'

'I see. Well, the Diaspora,' she says. 'Let me ask you, Rico. Are you single?'

'Single, *sí*!'

'That's great. I'm after a single man, see, Rico? And they're so hard to find. So you've never been married? Or are you divorced? Not that it matters, in the long run.'

'Married, *sí*!'

'You were married?'

'Married, *sí*!'

'And how long ago was that?'

'What I win? I win somethin'?'

'No, no, Rico. Listen. I'm calling to say that if you're single and if you'd like to share some thoughts about anti-intellectualism in America, you know, maybe you and I could get together. Have a date. Do you ever get up to Massachusetts? Hello?'

SCHÖNE WORTE MACHEN DEN KOHL NICHT FETT, isn't that what might be said? Fine words don't grease a cabbage? She's no expert in this German business – if her life depended on it she'd be dead already, if it meant she'd have to know a lot of German. It's not a natural language for small dark manic people like herself to speak. It gives them nightmares and delusions. DER SCHÖNE PLAN IST INS WASSER GEFALLEN, looks like; maybe. My gorgeous plan is going down Niagara in a barrel:

Raymond Kafka: married.

Norman Kafka: hangs up.

Norbert Kafka: ditto.

Marty Kafka: 'Actually, yes. I am, yes. A *confirmed* bachelor, if you want the truth.'

'Like a "confirmed" reservation, huh, Marty?' Fran jokes. 'That's a little joke. That's a little levity. *Of course* I know what time it is.'

'Well, what kind of survey is this, Miss Koslow? I don't want you to think I'm being rude, but –'

'It's Doctor. Doctor Koslow. Fran Koslow, pee-aitch-dee.'

'I don't get too many women calling from New England at one-thirty in the morning to ask me if I'm single.'

'Well, that's what makes me special, Marty.'

'I beg your pardon?'

'That I'd call you up at one-thirty in the morning sight unseen just to ask you for a date.'

'I think that makes you *crazy*, Dr Koslow.'

'Oh, no, no, no. Not crazy, Mr Kafka. No, no, no. I have a *schöne plan*. I want to marry someone with the last name "Kafka".'

'Is this a joke?'

'Not at all.'

'Did my mother put you up to this?'

'I don't even know your mother. Yet.'

'What are you, *nuts*?'

'Well, think about it.'

'*Think* about it?'

''Cause then I'd be Fran Kafka.'

''Cause then you'd be . . . Fran Kafka.'

'Sure.'

''Cause then you'd be *Fran Kafka*? Why don't you try to marry someone called *Cis of Assisi* while you're at it, too? Huh? Get it? "Cis of Assisi"? Huh? *Fran* Cis of Assisi –? Or how 'bout, how 'bout, "Klee Lady, I don't give a damn"? Huh? How 'bout that? As in *Fran* Klee Lady, I don't give a good God damn –'

She draws an extra heavy thick pen line through Marty Kafka's name and Marty Kafka's number, leaving only Kenneth Kafka, Gil and Barry Kafkas yet to go.

She's used to disappointment. After all, searching for a husband by telephone is hard enough; searching for a *Kafka* husband in this way is very nearly impossible. Especially since she can use the phone with freedom only in these bleak late hours after Sherm and Dina are asleep, when there are howlings in the street, when one must draw in, make a circle 'round oneself, when it isn't safe to stand and look from windows anymore. They are all around, this time of night. They are on the black roofs, in the alleys, in the shadows of the doorways. People know that they are there, so people draw into these shelters, these closed circles 'til the dawn, another morning. There is nothing anyone can do except pull in, stay away from the perimeter, and hide.

'Have you ever read the "K" words in the dictionary?' Fran once asked a Kafka in L.A., befoe he hung up on her. 'I have. Because I have a "K" name, same as you. I've read them. And you know what? "K" words are the ghetto of the English language. All of them are foreigners: Hindi, Russian, Scottish, German, Arabic, Jewish, Japanese. You know how many words you have to read through in the "K" section of the dictionary before you come to one that's American? Nineteen. Nineteen – in Webster's dictionary! And you know what word it is? *Kachina*. Like in *Kachina doll*. It's Hopi. The next American word after that is "Kalamazoo". The first English, totally *English* word is "kale". That's like on the second page, fifth column of the "K" words in use in the English language, already, you know what I mean? Hello? Hello?'

. . . Kenneth Kafka: line's disconnected.

. . . Gilbert Kafka: female answers.

. . . Barry Kafka.

Gott in Himmel, this Barry Kafka could be the ol' *Topf* of *Gold*. For one thing he doesn't hang up right away. And he's single. He sounds very nice. He doesn't ask if she knows what time it is. He gives thought to his answers, weighs her questions:

'So let me ask you, Barry. You sound so nice. What part of the world does your family come from?'

'The Middle.'

'A perfect answer.'

'No . . . let me change that. The Fringe.'

'Even better.'

'No . . . let me change that again. I was right the first time. We come from The Middle.'

'Barry Kafka! May I tell you, Barry Kafka, this is Love?'

'Sure. Go ahead.'

'Or do you hold, as Schopenhauer did, and later Nietzsche, that existence as we can experience it is merely a result of a blind force that the will consists in, and that optimism – and, consequently, Love – is an immoral way of thinking?'

'Sure, well . . . I could play with that.'

'Yes? Of course there are those who say Schopenhauer stole

his best thought from Kant, but what's not derivative, huh, Barry? What the hell ever fell *new* from the sky? Can you tell me? You remember how Schopenhauer epitomized his notion of moral Wrong? Cannibalism. Yes, Barry. He epitomized Wrong as cannibalism. When one's will is eaten. And remember what Levi-Strauss said about Culture? I think these concepts synchronize – Love, Morality, Culture – Levi-Strauss says Culture begins, it *begins*, Barry, Culture begins where incest is outlawed ...'

'*Incest?*'

'Culture begins where it's outlawed.'

'You mean sex with a mother and son?'

'Or a sister and brother, don't forget, Barry. As in the case of the Pharaohs.'

'*Levi-Strauss* said that?'

'*Le même*,' Fran jokes.

'The blue jeans guy?'

'*Blue* genes?' Fran repeats: 'What a clever way with words you have –!

'Barry?'

'Yeah?'

'I feel we're getting very close.'

'Are we . . . are you starting now?'

'Starting?'

'Are we going to play it as "Incest"? I've, uh, never played the incest mode, but what the hell, I'm game. Why don't you start. Go ahead. Uh, play the Mother. Talk dirty, too. I like that. Talk about cats fucking. Talk fucking filthy dirty to me, Mommy . . .'

Fran senses something moving in the hallway.

'Barry?' she whispers, terrified.

'Yes, Mom?'

She can hear him breathing.

Stealthily the hand of a glimpsed form falls noiselessly across the cradle of the telephone receiver and the silence holding Fran to Barry Kafka is transposed into another higher range of silence, one which threatens with each moment to burst into a howl, a savage war cry.

Dina takes the phone from Fran. She moves across the kitchen in her barefeet and draws herself a glass of water from the tap. She moves as if she's tracking something. She doesn't speak to Fran. She takes a sip of water. Her bathrobe smells of sex. She looks at Fran and finally says, 'Have you completely lost your mind?'

They seem to stare at one another although Fran, herself, is looking less at Dina than at the *distance* that the walls define, the way they seem to form a ring around their voices. 'Don't talk so loud,' Fran whispers.

Dina puts her glass down on the counter with a force that cracks it. 'I'll talk any way I goddam please. The phone bill came today.'

Except for tracing interlocking circles with her finger on the tabletop, Fran holds very still.

'Who the *hell* have you been calling?'

'No one.'

'Answer, Fran. I've had to take a lot of shit from Sherman over this. The bill is seven hundred dollars.'

'I'll pay you back.'

'The hell you'll pay us *back*: you'll *pay* it. Now. Tonight. Or else you're packing.'

'I don't have the money.'

'Did you go to that employment office?'

'Yes.'

'Don't lie to me! I called there myself! I know you didn't!'

Fran continues to draw circles on the tabletop.

'I'm working on my resumé,' she whispers.

'No one gives a fuck about your resumé! No one gives a fuck about your PhD! No one gives a fuck about your thesis, do you understand?'

Fran doesn't move.

In the middle of the night the best plan, *der best-plan*, is to pull in, make a circle, keep one's head down low.

'You have to go,' Dina finally dictates.

'Let me spend the night,' Fran pleads. 'I'll make some calls . . .'

'No more calls!'

'Only just a couple . . .'

'*No.*'

'You want me to be killed.'

'I just want you to *go away.*'

'I'm not prepared.'

'That's tough.'

'They'll kill me.'

'Fran . . .'

'They'll kill me, Dina. Can't you hear them? There are Indians out there.'

3 Geniuses

I

Saint Aquinas in the Kitchen

This morning a guy comes in, he says he'll have 'blueberry pancakes'.

I says, 'Blueberry pancakes ain't on the menu.'

He says, 'It says here you have fresh pancakes and it says you have fresh blueberries so you throw the berries in the pancake batter, what's the big deal? See what you can do, okay, good-looking?'

So I says, 'Sure.' I says, 'I'll see what I can do.'

I mean, I take a lot of lip, you know? I mean, a certain kind of lip I know I have to take but when it's 9.35 a.m. and I've been dishing eggs since five, don't call me 'good-looking'. I mean,

I've been *up* already for six hours so don't sweet-and-low the used goods, got it?

So right away I'm not exactly thrilled with Table Twelve, you understand. But I'm professional. People always give me nine-and-one-half for profession-ality. So I go to Dean back in the kitchen and I say, 'Some guy out here wants blueberry pancakes.'

'Tough shit,' Dean says.

'He says we've got the pancake batter and we've got the berries and he says we could combine the two.'

'You tell him,' Dean says, 'the cook sends him this.' (A finger.) 'And this . . .' (The finger, sideways.) 'For his *cat*,' Dean says.

'No go,' is what I say to Table Twelve.

'Oh come on, cutie-pie. I got my mouth set up for it. Go back there and do them up for me yourself, how 'bout it, special, just for me –?'

'Sure thing,' I says.

I mean, by this time this guy has got my colon in an uproar.

'You want eggs with those?'

'Sure. Eggs.'

'Two smilin' at 'ya?'

'Sure.'

'With patties?'

'Sure. Some patties. Bacon, too. A little extra bacon. You know. Just a slice or two, because you're back there. You don't have to put it on the bill, or nothin', sweetheart . . .'

You hear some awful stories, you know, about guys *urinating* on the food if someone sends it back; but sometimes, let me tell you, people are disgusting, plain disgusting, in the way they treat you.

'Where's my pancakes?' this guy says to me a little later.

'You want more?' I ask him.

'More? What *more*? You didn't bring me none –'

'What's *this*, then?'

I shove an empty plate from off the kitchen dolly in his face. It has a little pool of maple syrup on one side.

'You *ate* them,' I explain.

'No I didn't.'

'Go on, don't jerk with me, I've been a waitress sixteen years –'

'I ate them?' he asks and rolls his eyes.

'Sure,' I tell him. 'Then I brought the eggs.'

'I *ate* blueberry pancakes?'

'Well, here's the empty plate. You want some more?'

'No, no, that much was plenty . . .'

'And you *liked* them, too. You said, "Honey, you sure do make a yummy pancake," and I said, "Well, Jack, just so long as I can keep the customer content . . ."'

I mean, it took more than a little native talent to convince the man he'd eaten something which he hadn't. Got me two-sixty, though, plus what it added to the total tip. I mean, Dean is a mean son-of-a-bitch, but what the hell, I split it with him. A dollar these days is a dollar, you know? Good-lookin' or no good-lookin', I says if it falls on your plate on the way to someone else's mouth, you either got to pass it off, or eat it.

2

Isaac Newton in Nairobi

In the hut there's Rima, me and Pirou – Pirou in for the first time.

Last time was me and Rima and the woman Neefa. Neefa in for few days. She like crocodile with her big snout. She don't know it, how I learn to count.

I start counting long ago in days that live behind the shoulder. Mamaliha call these *water* days. They live like sky and trees on water, break in circles when you try to dish their pictures out. I ten summers old, but those times I don't count, don't count, don't *begin* to count, can't count, can't understand. Mamaliha saying one two three four on her fingers but I see nothing there except for Mama's fingers, tree bark brown.

She laugh.

She laugh, her yellow mouth.

They call me Rookoo, sound of stupid bird.

I come first time to the hut a full round moon.

I come again, a moon again, same women with me. We have some talk. I never heard such talk. Sika, she the barren woman, how they punish her. They make her sit alone. They make her sit in same place in the dirt and when she leave they spit on the place and no one ever sit there on the hole that's Sika's place.

After Sika's husband die his brother takes her and they make the little baby Pirou and Sika she not barren anymore. All the women from the hut drink dirt tea, show their shame. Mamaliha tell me never to make words like arrows, like the other women. I make silence. I make silence at my men, but that okay. Silence at the bottom of the river, where the claw waits. Silence at the bottom of the tree root, too, beneath the brown tree bark.

I start looking all around to see who comes in the hut. Some women this time, other women different time, and different women. I wonder. Different times and different women.

Strange thing: full round moon and me don't always go to hut together. Moon fall way behind. So I keep stick.

Stick I bite each morning, hide inside my mat in corner. Full round moon, I take new stick.

Many sticks.

Long, long days ago, like stars over the shoulder.

Many stars.

They call me Rookoo the Wisewoman.

This I'm saying: she the stupid bird, who see only things that sit before her eyes. But she the Wisebird who can see in dark the written law of nature.

3

Alexander Bell in Brooklyn

What *is* it? she screams at me.

'It's an *amphora*! You don't know what an *amphora* is? Dummy! It's a clay pot! You know what they used to keep in these clay pots? Everything! You know where this clay pot comes from? Cairo! You know who brought this clay pot back from Cairo? My father's father's uncle's uncle, that's who! You know why? Because God's Voice is on here! Put a needle in this groove. Run a needle right through here. Listen. Here that? God's Voice! Is That a Voice?! What a Voice He had!'

She's *deaf*, I'm thinking. The woman's crazy old and *deaf*, and now she wants to pawn this pot. This pot has got to be the last proverbial you-know-what – I mean, the one that when *it* goes she won't have one to diddle in.

'What'll you offer?' she shouts at me.

Twenty bucks, I say.

'*Twenty bucks?*' she yells. She must have read my lips: 'Twenty lousy *bucks?* For God's Voice? The One and Only? From your lousy lips to His Ears! You hear this, God?' she shouts at the ceiling. 'You hear what kind of things are going on down here?'

Twenty bucks, take it or leave it, I say.

'He says, "Twenty-five," you got yourself a deal!' she shouts.

Twenty-two-fifty, I say. And that's my final offer.

'What do you think you know from "final"?' she demands. 'Crook! I'll take it! From Cairo and from God's Lips! You should rejoice in such a deal!'

I should rejoice?

Madam, I beg of her, Who am I to play the skeptic? You want me to Rejoice? I promise to Rejoice: Break a little bread. Take a little tipple. Pay the little taxes.

'Dummy!' she yells: 'Not me! *God* wants you to rejoice! It's what *He* wants! What?!' she hollers at the ceiling:

'He says He wants it paid in silver!'

In silver? I repeat.

'Silver dollars!' she demands.

'Lady, I don't *have* that many silver dollars. They don't *make* that many silver dollars, anymore.'

'Crook!' she hollers.

'This is the last time you cheat *Him*!' she yells. 'You wait and see!' She leaves.

Well what does she think *she* knows?

What does she mean, the last time I'll cheat *Him*?

What does she think *she* knows from 'last'?

I've got the pot: the *amphora*.

The I-should-only-tell-you-from-my-lips-to-God's-own-Ears so-called priceless antiquity.

Three hundred dollars.

No.

Nine thousand dollars.

No.

'Too plain.'

'A nice red pot.'

'What are all these *grooves*?'

For you: *two* hundred dollars.

'Two hundred dollars!' this man in this nice suit is shouting at me. 'Do you know what you *have* here?! This is a *priceless antiquity*!'

It *is*?

'With these important grooves!'

Important –?

'*Grooves!* Do you know what these mean?!'

In *Braille*? I ask.

'The strong – and I mean strong! – the strong pos-si-bil-i-ty of the *recording* hereupon of *voices*!'

Voices?

'Words! Thoughts! Ideas, man! Greetings! Salutations! Messages!'

Has everyone gone *deaf*?

Why are they all *shouting*?

You're the second person in a row to hint at that, I mention.

He seems to watch my lips move.

Do I imagine that he seems to watch my lips move?

'Just last week!' he shouts. 'At Carnegie Hall! They had a vase there that spoke Latin!'

They *did*? I inquire.

'This potter!' he shouts. 'This potter back in 56 AD! He was watch-callit: throwing a pot! And his stylo accidentally inscribed this groove! And just then his friend called out, "Hey, Octavio! Are you goin' to the baths tonight?" in *Latin*, man! But in the *real* Latin, like in the Latin that was *spoken* not just *handed down*! And the sound of that was caught, man, on that *vase*! The sound of that was *caught*! Right there! And all they had to do was turn it *back*, man, at the right rotation! I mean, at the certain right-on-target *rate* of rotation and voilà! *Latin*, man! A goddam recording! And you got yourself the Real McCoy here by the looks of it! Just like last week at Carnegie Hall! They sold out! Yes, indeedy! They sold out to hear, "Hey, Octavio!" in the *true gen*! Well it was worth it! Was it not worth every cent? What do you say? Is it not worth every *sou* to hear real Latin?!'

Well, I suppose so.

'You *suppose* so! You could have ancient Greek right here! You could have Phoenician! No one speaks Phoenician these days! You could have Assyrian or Babylonian! You could have the language of Atlantis, for godsake –!'

Well, actually, I'm told it is the Master's Voice.

'No kidding!'

Yes. God's.

'Well, this is worth a *fortune*, man! This is a gold mine! This could be the Covenant Update! Let's see if we can make it talk! What do you say? Do you have a lazy Susan or a lathe or anything laying around that *turns*?!'

It's *mine*, I hear myself tell him.

I almost can't believe the sound of my own words:

Take your hands off my amphora! Take your business and your rumors elsewhere!

'"*Rumors*"?!' he protests.

Get out! I holler.

'But "*rumors*," man?!'

Get out! Get out! Get out!

I pick up the pot and run it and the man in this nice suit outside onto the sidewalk. Mrs Neidermeyer's passing by, and Mrs Wong with her shopping cart that has the wobbly wheel. These women talk my ears off every chance they get.

Shut up! I scream.

You shut up and *you* shut up and *you* shut up and *you* shut up, I holler at them. I don't want to hear another word!

I lift the pot with both hands above my head and pitch it onto Atlantic Avenue. It doesn't break apart until the bus for Sheepshead Bay runs over it and the shards fly off ferociously in all directions like clay pigeons at a practice shoot, and then they all stop talking, all at once.

The clear blue sky.

The world has been as silent as the inside of a bell jar, ever since.

Green Park

There is a park in London bounded by two palaces, kept green in every season by the seeds of envy scattered by an angry queen. Her name was Catherine. She was Portuguese by birth, transplanted like a hothouse shoot onto a bleak heathriddled shore where she was mortgaged to the King of England without interest, where she bore no arguable reason not to be forgotten in the scope of Anglo-Saxon history, although her husband's mistresses bore thirteen different ones among them. She, alone, among the many women that he bedded, remained barren. No heir took root within her womb. She was not immortalized, as wives of kings should be, by having mothered sovereigns. She is not remembered by the lovers strolling in this park, by the couples kissing on iron benches under sycamores, by the dreamers lying in each other's arms in public on the grass at mid-day, as if the secrecy, itself, of assignations such as these must cloak, mist-like, the truth, disguise the infidelities. Only History renders the condition of invisibility, not Love; and yet these lovers act as if no one can see them. They slide their hands beneath their lovers' coats, they wrap their legs around each other and they never, not once, entertain a thought about the queen named Catherine nor wonder why it is that of the many parks in London, this one has no pond; it has no slow seductive cresting contemplative body of grey water: And it bears no flowers. None.

There were none who noticed them when they met every evening in Green Park, their names will be unknown, their love will be forgotten, and the piquancy of them will go to loam. Beneath the sycamores or under shared umbrellas, they spent hours every evening, talking. When they kissed, they kissed with their mouths open. His lips made propositions to her of an act to be performed. His hands were parables; his touch was propaganda. But what is romance if not the spore of the improbable, a score of black swans flying through one's dreams? He knew that if he followed on his impulse, if he fell in love with her, then reality would change. *Garnet* would no longer be a color, but an act. *Cat* would be a project of suspension. The single syllable of *sash* would sound alarm. All the rivets of his universe would come to dust, and trust, that scholar in the pasteboard cap, that fop, that slop jar at the backdoor of one's reason, would have been betrayed for passion. He was married to another woman, and he made for himself religions of a modern man: a wife, a house, a garden, job, his children. He loved her and desired her and wanted her, but: in the evenings he went home. His seasons passed between two women, both of whom he loved, until the physics of deception wore him thin. 'Please, understand,' he begged his lover. And she did. She didn't call. She didn't give in to the weakness of demanding a last scene, of demanding explanation when he left her standing in Green Park. He didn't call. Some afternoons he stared into his hands or watched the telephone. He thought he smelled her perfume in his home. He lay in bed at night next to his wife and closed his eyes and tried not seeing the brown nebulae around his lover's nipples, nor the little stars that shone within her skin. For weeks he launched tin soldiers in a battle on the flat remembered plain that was her abdomen, denying to himself that what he had to do was act dead, or surrender. He refused to think her name. He tried to keep her particles suspended in a hidden place, but the elements producing tempest cannot stop themselves. Fragrance cannot stop itself. A fire can't, nor tides, nor prayers dispatched to heaven. What is started will complete itself, despite one's intervention. He invented distance, he invented every reason not to want to touch her then he showed up late one night outside her door. She took him in.

The legend errs, the legend asks us to believe that Love cuts both ways, double-bladed, one edge smooth and painless as compassion, one edge vicious as revenge:

'Where do you start?'

'Where do *I* start?'

'Where does . . . a woman start to shave herself?' he asks.

He sits on the edge of her bath; she reclines the nape of her neck on the curve of the porcelain. Green and red facets of bubble bath glisten.

'How does a man shave?' she asks.

'*Standing up*,' she is told.

She clears a flotilla of bubbles away and raises an elbow, exposing her breast.

'Start with the underarm,' she suggests.

He wavers: 'Up or down?'

'Doesn't matter, just follow the contour.'

He soaps the shaving brush, then dabs the lather with

painterly carefulness onto her canvas. She watches him, and he studies his work. He picks up the razor.

'The hairs are so tiny,' he says. 'What if I nick you, just look at these veins.'

'A roadmap,' she says.

'Jesus, so blue. Don't even breathe,' he instructs.

The blade clears a path through the lather.

He rinses the razor.

'How was that, did it hurt?'

'Like a feather,' she says.

He rolls up his sleeve. With the care of a watchmaker he makes a move, then another. He rinses the razor. With the air of a prelate, he wipes her clean with a cloth.

'Next,' he says, smugly.

She raises her other arm, leans further back to make herself comfortable.

He soaps the brush.

To reach, he leans over her, presenting his face in its profile before her; presenting his ear to her mouth.

When he is finished he washes her shoulders and rinses the razor.

He sits on the edge of the tub with a towel on his knees.

'Next,' he says, very pleased with himself.

She raises a leg to his lap.

'See how the hairs grow?' she asks.

He holds her leg in his hands.

'In a pattern,' he says.

'No, *down*,' she instructs him, 'so you have to shave *up*.'

'But in a pattern,' he marvels, again.

He traces the hairs of her leg with the palms of his hands. The hairs lay like runes on her skin, running around the smooth muscle, as if they'd been turned on a clay-potter's wheel. The long narrow groove defined by her tibia glistens; it's hairless. The back of her knee joint is smooth.

'Amazing,' he says.

He lathers her calf and her ankle. He lathers her knee. Above her patella her skin stretches, hairless.

'And God made smooth thighs,' he intones.

'God was an Artist.'

'Don't talk,' he commands.

He begins with the blade at the ball of her ankle. There are three tiny hairs on her tarsus.

'Even *God* talked, you know,' she reminds him: 'Now and then . . .'

'He was lonely. He had to,' he says.

He rinses the razor.

'Can't you talk and shave women, both, at the same time?'

'I can't talk and shave *you* at the same time,' he says.

'I think we should talk. I think we should talk about what we have done to each other.'

'Don't move so much, darling,' he cautions.

He shaves her.

She watches.

The legend of Green Park, where he had once left her standing, is that Queen Catherine, the Portuguese, on learning her husband was using the park as a garden to grow bright red roses and poppies to send to his mistresses, had them torn out and salted their earth and outlawed the growing of flowers. It is only a myth. It is only a myth to explain why the ground is called Green:

'I thought I'd lost you,' she says. 'I thought you weren't coming back.'

'So did I.'

'Are you back?'

'Well, I'm here . . .'

'Look at me! Are you back?'

For a moment it seems they might love one another enough to forgive.

'I couldn't stop dreaming of you.' He wipes her leg clean with the cloth and inspects it. He kisses her instep. '*Next*,' he whispers.

She slides her leg from his knees, shifting her weight on her hips to reverse in the water. Waves lap at fjords, archipelagos drift and collide and reform in the tub, making mountains which wink with the light. He soaps the brush. She gives him her unshaven leg. He lathers the length of it; then he picks up the razor.

'Weekends were the worst,' he explains. 'We put in the garden. I gardened like hell to forget you.'

There is an instant when she might have said that he's cut her.

'White floribundas for Jan,' he goes on.

She scoops up some bubbles to cover the scar.

'Tea roses for me, "Whiskey Mac's", purple leaves, amber flowers. Three rambler roses, the "Albéric Barbiers", apple-scented, to remind me of you.'

'Sounds dreamy.' She tries to sound steady. 'What color?'

'Cream-white.'

'Stunning by moonlight,' she says.

He works with delicate strokes 'round her ankle.

'While I was planting the roses, I dreamed them in bloom. In moonlight.' He smiles. 'Smelling like apples. You had your hair up. We were dancing,' he says.

'Very slow?'

'Hardly moving.'

'A violin?'

'Clarinet.'

'Where was Jan?'

He hesitates, making a quick, final stroke.

'Jan was . . . she didn't exist.'

He washes her leg with the cloth.

He places the razor on the edge of the tub, dries his hands.

'Join me?' she asks.

He nods and stands up.

'I'll bring us some wine,' he says.

'Good idea,' she answers.

'Vouvray?'

'A claret. And turn on some music?' she begs.

She lowers her leg.

She lights the candles next to the bath, her hands dripping water. The shadows play over her skin. She opens the hot water tap and adds bubbling crystals. A tongue of steam rises and teases the mirror. Strains of a cello *andante* begin. She foments the water to stir up the bubbles and sees it, red ribbon, a bright racine vine in the water, a shimmering curtain, her blood, unfurling itself like a shoot, turning the water not crimson or brilliant, but soft pink and pearly and rose.

'It still needs more color,' he says.

He hands her a stem of the claret, resting his glass on the edge of the tub, near the razor. He starts to undress.

'I'm sorry –?'

'The garden.'

'Oh. Yes.'

'Not a riot. A touch. A blush, here and there. A suggestion of red.'

She raises her glass, tips a stream of dark wine down her belly.

'A suggestion of red would be perfect,' she says.

He lowers himself.

They face one another. A ruby lagoon lies between them. A cello is playing somewhere. Hibiscus is blooming. A kingfisher cries.

She toys with the razor. It glistens. A riot of color.

'Next?' she suggests.

Not owning a trowel, she had taken a knife from the kitchen.

He had made her suffer silence, suffer silence like a small death.

From where do ultimatums spring? Is there a forest of them, white and tight as fiddleheads, blanched and lacking passion in a field of green?

Do this, or else do that.

Love or don't. Stop it.

Walk this way.

Pedestrians proceed on 'green'.

In the face of it what was she to do but spend the winter reading Tolstoy, spend the summer-after-next obsessed, self-dramatizing. Often something started to remind her of him and she snuffed it out, outlawed it in the land; then somehow she had managed to survive a weekend.

Sundays in the city without loving him: the architecture had been very changed, very much conditional to the status of *outside*: come in, go out, come back, please stay, please love, forever; effortlessly.

So someone dies within the city, in another suburb, someone's face turns red and she falls over, so what, what of it, people all around are dying silent airless deaths each day, who cares if one sad silly lonely woman throws herself onto a motorway from a footbridge?

Imagine the surprise to the unassuming motorist.

Are there words that have no opposites?

What is the opposite of unrequited?

In the days after he had left her she kept thinking, 'This won't last. This silence will not last. A silence cannot last forever.'

In the weeks following his departure, she had felt a tunnelling amass, a tunnel of the unrequitable, a sound of a black water dripping; torture.

At night she had walked the city, taking his train line south to Green Park, standing on the platform of the Undergound, thinking she could accidentally put herself before his path. She had walked into Trafalgar Square, to the Embankment, over the Thames to the South Bank across the Hungerford Bridge, shared by trains. To her left St Paul's Cathedral had loomed, never looking the same color twice; on her right, Westminster; beneath her, the mutable Thames, like a lust.

The sodium lamps made the sky look like rust.

Some nights she had sat on a bench on the South Bank and stared over the water at the city and dared it to hide him from her.

But a city like London has a resistance to dares. A city like London states its defiance in silence.

What is another small death in a city of millions of people?

The river, the trains, the trains and the river, the buses, the parks: at night she kept moving.

She had walked through the Horse Guards Parade, where the cobblestones smelled of manure.

She had walked to the mosque in St John's Wood where, on the east side of the building, there was the strange smell of smoke.

She had walked into mews, along alleyways, listening, always, for some susurration, for someone to call in an audible voice, for someone to whisper her name.

The silence was numbing, like sleeping on ice.

She forgot how to talk.

She had listened and watched, she had looked and had listened; she'd walked, watching others. She, and the millions of others. She had hidden the knife in her coat.

When he consigned her to silence, when he had condemned her to that realm, that unutterable tamping, when he had issued his silent imperative, she had decided to scream, tear tooth and nail at its seamlessness, die, rage, murder, wound, explode, so she'd sat on a bench in Green Park with the bulbs in a bag after dark, choosing her targets, telling herself, 'It was *here*, it was *here*, it was *here*, yes, you fucker, London, knife in the earth, it was *here* where we loved.'

Fifty-five bulbs.

Fifty-five holes on the earth: you'll see, you'll see, you will see it here, damn you, you bastard, what one angry woman can do.

He had said, 'You'll survive. You have the gift to be lonely.'
You may as well go tell the dead they know how to be lonely.
You may as well go tell the dead they know how to be dead.
Go tell the dead they know how to be dead.
Go tell the dead they know how to be lonely.
Go tell these flowers how not to exist.

Quicksand

Information travels on a circuit, same as jurisprudence in the Old West, same as uninvited preachers of the Word who ride up in the night in black coats, tie their nags outside your window, watch and wait. Information lays in store for you. With the morning, with the coming of the dawn, through the post, from a stranger, at a corner or by accident, you learn more than you want to know. You learn that facts are backed by guarantees. You learn the secrets of success and of the stars. You learn that everything in nature owns a sound. You learn to keep your vigilance among the sounds that come at night. You learn to recognize the semi-quavers in her breathing. You learn to listen for the ring of truth in what she'll say. You yearn to keep the information undisclosed that the person laying next to you is lying.

*

We were driving fast through France late one night in February, when it started snowing. We hadn't spoken for an hour. It began to snow, solitary flakes, as big as dandelions. We passed a sign which told us we were heading toward 'TOULOUSE-ESPAGNE'.

'The taller brother of,' she joked.

Snowflakes, broad as Van Gogh's brush strokes, sped into the yellow circle of our headlights like iron filings 'round a magnet. The speed at which they flew at us was terrifying.

'I'm pulling over.'

'Don't,' she said.

'You drive, then.'

'No. Keep going.'

'Can't see.'

'It doesn't matter.'

'Can't see the fucking *road*.'

She unhitched her safety harness.

She took off her coat.

'Fanny?'

'Just keep driving, Tom.'

She took her sweater off and then her blouse. She rolled her window down. Snowflakes flew onto her shoulders.

'Fucking Christ,' I said.

I pulled off the road and she got out and ran.

From the darkness twelve feet down the road, she stepped into the cone cast by the headlights. She was facing me.

Twenty minutes later, when the snow had stopped and we were on the road again, I asked her, 'What the hell was *that* about?'

'You had your chance,' she said.

'For what?'

She didn't answer.

'For *what*, for christsake?'

She didn't speak again until the gendarme at the border asked if we had something to declare.

'Absolutely nothing,' Fanny said in plain flat English.

She's an art historian and in her conversation her training in art history shows. You hear the sounds of someone steeped in the belief that art is a continuum through Time, existing outside ordinary Life. She is extraordinary in the way that she succeeds in using words to talk about a thing whose sound is heard by seeing. *There is a moment just behind the knee,* she can say about a Degas nude, *where the silhouette is almost disappearing.*
Her name is Fanny.
She's my wife.

'I'll take all the blame for this,' she says.
She's in control again but anyone can see that she's been crying. Richard takes one look at her, standing at the door, and tries his best to smooth out his reaction. 'Aha,' he says. 'No wonder you're an hour late.' He kisses Fanny with the absent-mindedness that twenty years' habituation can instill. 'You look fucking awful, darling. What have you been up to?'
'I'm sorry we're so late,' she says. 'It's all my fault.' She stares down at his hand where he has placed it on her arm.
'If it's sympathy you're after, you'll find none in here,' he says. 'Just a viper's nest of all my very dearest friends.'
'All one of them?'
'But darling, there are *two* of you.'
'Do married couples rate as one or two these days? Or do they rate as three? Three is such a busy little number. One plus two is three. Or maybe man and wife just rate as zero nowadays.'
She is wound as tight as a propeller on a young boy's model airplane.
'Don't spoil my little party, Fanny,' Richard asks her gently.
'Have I ever?'
'No.'

'You lying fuck.' She picks his hand off her as if it were a slug.
'May I present my husband? Richard this is Tom. Tom, meet
Richard. You fellas ought to have a lot in common. Now point
me toward the brandy, will you, baby?'

There is a moment just behind her knee where I know her flesh
deceives me. 'Like the skin of Cézanne's apples,' she is saying.
'What is?' someone asks.
We are all a little tired and a little drunk.
'Truth,' she says.
'Oh fuck truth. Fu-uck Truth. Fuh-uh-uh-uck *Truth*. That's
what I say . . .'
'Well said.'
'There is no Truth. Truth died, 1848. I have it from on-High,
before *He* died, oh yes. Before *He* died He wrote my great-great-
grandfather the rabbi an inter-Office memo. "Fuck Truth", it
said. "Truth died last year. It will have *always* died last year."
Last year it died in Bhopal. The year before, in Ethiopia. The
year before that, in Pretoria. The year before, it died –'
'Are you saying Truth goes to the Third World every year
like a salmon just to spawn and die?'
'. . . Am I saying? Am I saying that? I think more likely what
I'm saying is, we are jerks and assholes and Truth, 'though
dead, is always dying.'
'True.'
'God bless. So wherzit dying?'
'Where's it *dying*?'
'Wherzit dying *now*?'
'You mean . . . ?'
'Yeah, Truth. This year. Somewhere in the World. Where is
it dying?'
'In the bedroom,' someone says.
'Whose? Yours?'
'Fuck this conversation. "We interrupt this evening's News

142

of the Universe to bring you a live broadcast from the letters page of *Playboy*" . . .'

'Truth is dying in my *bedroom*,' Fanny says.

She's drunk.

Nobody's listening.

The first year we were married she explained to me an edge is seen with two eyes working on the same plane, but a curve will seem to roll away because our eyes must see it from two separate points in space. She used a rounded table napkin for her illustration. She also taught me facts of light: that textured surfaces project, flat ones receive. She said that every work of art deceives: it *must* deceive. Its success is, by its very nature, a deception. She made me promise on our honeymoon that we would try to make of marriage something that could come as close to being art as one can make of separate lives. And at many things we do succeed. We have friends, we have our shared experience. We have each other, spectrum's complements. She made me promise we would bring out all the best in one another, as blue for orange, and red for green; as yellow does for purple. Three. She tried to teach me there are three primary colors: that any two combined then complement the third. These are facts of light. There is the ring of truth about them. They are guaranteed not to deceive you. You can trust them.

'Til the dark.

'Tom?'

She has the faintest whisper.

I feel her breath against my skin.

'Are you awake?'

I don't want to tell her, if I am.

I don't want to start the conversation that I know is coming.

She gets up to draw the curtain back a little, naked woman in blue moonlight.

As she stands there, there's a moment just behind her spine which says *she knows*. It says she owns the information. She holds the news, the silhouetting line along her spine is tense with it. She knows she must apply it with precision and great tact, as if it were the final stroke of lucid color to a finished canvas. But the facts of lying vibrate silence. She would have to crack the dome to speak the truth, and even if she did, the fact of lying is that it perpetuates itself. It never ends. It ravels in the mind. It produces its own echo in a place of utter silence. It weights you from within, conceives a gravity by which, even in your dreams, you sense your constant slow descent.

'Tom?'

If I could will her not to ask what she is going to ask, I would.

'Level with me,' Fanny says.

There was a season when the three of us had two best friends among the others. Richard and I were freestyle swimmers, Fanny was the diver. We were always either in the pool or thinking about traveling through water. Fanny timed us, sometimes, in the evenings, and we spotted for her. Her hair was very short back then, as it had to be. She wore a towel around her neck. Our voices echoed in the walls. When she clocked us, she would jot our times in two matched columns on a clipboard. The times were to the millisecond. Fanny wore the whistle.

'That night when we were driving through the snow in France,' she says. 'The way the snow looked, falling, was the way it used to feel. Diving into fireworks, into a chrysanthemum, right into its center, falling. Do you understand?'

'Yes.'

'Good. You should have run me over.'

'Why would I want to do a thing like that?'

She takes a breath, then steadies; preparation.

Once we take these steps we'll have to fall.

Even at this edge she must be thinking, *Stop us now, before we do it.*

144

'I used to think it had to be another woman. That shows you
how completely fucked I was.'

One can hear but one can't answer, underwater.

One can see but one can't run towards shore.

'It's not another woman, is it, Tom?'

'I don't know what you're –'

'*Is* it, Tom?'

'– accusing me of.'

'Get out of bed.'

'I can't.'

'Get out.'

'I am.'

'Get out.'

'I'm trying.'

'Try a whole lot faster, lying fuck! The two of you are lying
bastard fucks!'

Then let me die from laughter, Fanny, but the lie is what
we've held to all these years. One twisted lie to save us all from
drowning. One pathetic twisted rotten scabrous *root*.

Pleasure

On the beach there were two women wrapped in white (or so it had appeared); two dogs; and several children. Behind the women on the beach the russet bluffs rose, cosseting the dusty miller and the random vines. The shoreline was decaying. The clay that held the roots that held the shore was slipping to the sea like lava from the lip of an inferno. Whole masses of topography had disappeared from one storm season to the next and the shore stood outlined in cross-section. Throughout its crumbling mass the ancient mollusks surfaced, the remains of kitchen middens riddled through the sinking loam like inky veins. Here, the history of the earth was nothing more than layers of compression which had failed to mass – the first could not support the last. The seeds were wasted. Overhead, the gulls were wheeling. Dark ocean boomed. The women wrapped in white turned their backs against the bluffs and faced the

149

wind. They called out to their children but the current off the
ocean forced their words away like kites, behind them. The
dogs raced after foam. The children ran among the boulders,
streaked with salt, exalted by the violent tide above their
ordinary gravity: they skittered and they floated through the
pale grey-yellow light. A shell upended on the spume, too
perfect on its axis in the sand for them to notice. They were
tossing seaweed at each other, devil's apronstrings. Their
hands were slimy with the gel of algae, their feet and limbs were
burnished by the sand. They laughed. They threw their heads
back and the muscles in their necks convulsed in laughter but
no sound escaped above the roar of the cold surf. The only
sound that mattered was the ocean, its rhythm marking time for
their emotions. Very late at night their burning minds would
still ring with its pounding. They would dream of underwater
worlds, of drowning and surviving where their silver bodies
knew no bounds within a silken seamless element, where no
sound escaped, no language issued but the constant lulling echo
of a single mournful song. The sea at bedtime is a sedative. By
day it is an incitation. In dreams it is consuming. Even children
guess its portent. Even children wake from nightmares, sound-
less, rigid, wet with sweat. In the ocean goes another way of
being. In the ocean is the other sex.

The women on the beach seemed more like statues than
women. They held themselves at pitch against the wind,
graceful, stony, resolute. The fabric of their white gowns
flapped and billowed in the wind, creating fantasies of flight
and incandescence 'round their bodies. They seemed the dis-
embodied figureheads of phantom bowsprits, the enigmatic
caryatids supporting portals of a lost dimension. One of them
was older than the other. One of them was taller. They were the
mothers of the children racing in the sand. They had known
each other several decades and each could sense the meaning in

the other's silence, in the other's glance. One of them was in great pain. She was the woman on the left, the taller of the two, the one on whom the catechism had been lost. She had never learned to forswear pleasures of the flesh. The woman on the right was different. She could sense, but she couldn't understand, the other's torment. Both of them were first to spot the fluke, before the children did, way out, at an incalculable distance, between the land where they were rooted, and the dark horizon. The women saw what seemed to be a large black bird across the distant water. The older of them raised her hand to shield her eyes and as she did, she saw the plume, rising like a white smoke on a valley morning from a cabin fire. The other woman saw it, too. Neither of them thought about a whale, they thought what they were used to thinking, what their minds had taught their eyes to see within a seasoned range of expectation: A monster could not surface from the deep. They were women in a panorama, statuesque, their children racing at their feet, their dogs delighted in their play and a monster could not surface from the deep before them, surely. No such thought occurred to them. They watched, transfixed, uncomprehending, as what they both perceived to be a bird and then a boat and then an oil rig gained in mass, increased and made toward shore, straight toward them. Slowly, like the rhythm of a sadness, sweet and tireless, the whale took form. Seeing only parts of it at first the women misconstrued it. Seeing only parts of it, in sequence, the women needed to imagine its completeness, its whole fluid self, the whale, half seen, half unseen, half-imagined, unmistakable. The children, racing with the tide, sensed the whale the way they sensed a storm or a disaster, and they stopped, together, all at once, and saw it. One of them thought it had come to take her from her mother and she, alone, was frightened. Her brother thought the whale had come to eat them. No one thought and no one knew, until they saw the blood inside its eye, that anything so wild, so huge, so massive could be powerless outside a given element. No one understood, until it happened, that the whale had beached itself with them to try to die.

There was no understanding its immensity. Its age and history and its sex were indecipherable. It could have been a meteor. It could have been a fallen planet, except it breathed. They had the feeling it was breathing. It didn't move and it was massive and the surf considered it another shore. The waves rolled in and broke across its dorsal. They thought it might be female by its stillness, then they thought it must be male because of size. Its head seemed half the length of its whole being. To see its face in full, they had to go away a great long distance. The younger children ran around its head, from eye to eye and back again, so it could see them, then they fell to touching it. Its skin was unresilient and hard, like touching a sequoia; its baleen, stiff and steamy. Its bones were filled with oil. No gravity had weighted it with marrow. Its body was a mass designed for motion and for song. Here was the behemoth, the leviathan, before them. The dogs were terrified; so were the women – less from fear than by the transformation of proportion, of reality, of sea and land and air and water, by the sudden stranding on the random cusp of a pertained existence of a thing, a creature that is one with humans in the nature of its blood, but outlawed at the gates of heaven, an animal that seemed to want to exercise a fatal act of will, who was, by accident, earth's largest creature. The women waded out to it, to come between it and their children. All around them wind ripped and the dogs' commotion kept the gulls at bay. 'Try to keep the dogs away!' the older woman shouted toward the children. The dogs were crouched into the surf beside the whale's left eye, snarling at it with their teeth bared. The black one backed away, giving a frustrated whimper at its mistress's command; but the tan one had to be restrained by her. That's when she saw the swelling. That's when she saw the blood inside its eye. The whale looked at her an instant. Then it turned its head. It dragged its head along the tideline and its baleen filled with sand. Out of water it looked ugly. It was pitted, barnacled and scarred, and yet the woman wanted to lay down with it. She put her palms against it, ran her hands along it, as a form of comfort. Instinctively the children tried to push it. They leaned against it with their shoulders and their backs and tried to push it back into the sea. They yelled at it as if it were a dog. 'Back!' they shouted. 'Back into the water, Mister Whaley!' The children didn't know a whale will drown in water when it cannot surface. But the women knew. The younger woman knew the whale was a phenomenon as major as an earthquake or a comet or a labor. The older woman knew the whale was not an earthquake, or a comet, or a labor. The whale was not a thousand things. The whale was dying. It had come because of her.

There's religion, there is love and there is passion; then there's a state of body and of mind that can invoke all three. It is neither love, alone; nor passion. It's a longing for another's limbs, it's sensing fingers through a fin or navigating through a realm of magic by one's skin. The younger woman thought the whale had swum off course or had been led into a trap by some misleading sign, the way a bird will fly into a plate glass window. She thought the situation could be fixed. The children thought the whale was sick. The older woman, only, understood the whale's displacement and its shame. She thought the whale had come to test her will. If she could overcome the web obsession weaves around a heart, if she could overcome her longing for the object of her love by an act of will, if she could move the whale into the water, then she could free herself, of pleasure.

She let the younger woman take the dogs and children down the beach to go find help. It was only when they were well beyond the range of hearing that she started speaking to the whale. She addressed it tentatively, whispering at first; then she heard herself adopting the convention of confession. She told the whale her secrets, told it how her body had betrayed her,

how her mind had been made prisoner of her sex. She spoke to it
of falling accidentally from an innocence to ecstasy, and then to
woe. She strung her life before the whale in words that shone
like rings of metal, links of mail. The whale listened to her. All
its strength seemed focused on the words the woman gave it. If
it slipped into the sea again it would have no strength to surface.
If it stayed exposed on shore, men would come and slice its skin,
and when it died it would pollute the sand on which it rested. It
listened to the woman and it watched her. All she seemed to
want from it was not to have to witness desecration. All she
seemed to beg was for the whale to slip away. She didn't beg a
miracle. All she begged was to preserve the thing that had been
beautiful. She whispered to it and it seemed to slip an inch, into
the water. She urged it and it moved. Its immensity went
slipping to the sea in inches. Its great tail hit the water and there
went up a sigh which sounded like a chute descending; the
waves crashed, and the whale was gone. The woman fought for
balance in the surf, fell, went under, and then ran toward shore.
She ran toward the high point on the beach, toward the bluffs.
She scanned the ocean. Nowhere on the surface of the sea in
front of her was there any shadow, any crest or break, a
footprint, any sign of it. She counted slowly, shivering, her wet
hair plastered to her shoulders, seconds, minutes, how much
time the whale would take to surface. She never wanted it to die.
Returned to its own element she hoped against all hope that it
could play again, its body built to frolic, its eyes and mind
designed for song and timeless motion. But into unseen depths
it sounded, staying down. The woman watched the surface,
frozen. When they saw her from a distance on the beach they
thought she looked more like a statue than a woman. They
came, bringing hooks and ropes and lines and motors. They
saw her standing with her back turned toward the bluffs, more
like a pillar than a woman. More like a stalagmite, crystalized
in air. A white pillar.

    Salt.

Among the Impressionists

For Lara

Lucy takes the number 159 bus to Trafalgar Square every day (except Easter and Christmas when state and religion dictate the closing of Room 44 at the National Gallery, where she goes to achieve an erotic experience). It's cozy there. They keep it quite nice. The people who clean it are careful. They do a good job.

Most women her age stay at home, watch the telly. Most women her age dream of men with compassion, like Jesus, who'll succour their ills. Some women her age long for men of brute force, which is fine, for those women, but Lucy is one who likes genius. She is a woman who warms to the men who can render a thunder, eternalise moments; the men who could make the earth move:

Some days it's Edgar – some days it starts with Degas. Either he or Renoir will get on the bus on the way to Trafalgar Square

157

and sit down beside her; the choice of companion depends on
the light. Some days it's Monet. Days when there's hardly a
sound and the streets and the sky are awash with clear grey, it's
Cézanne. Rarely does Manet climb onto the bus for a chat.
Rarely, too, does Pissarro. But today as the 159 bus turns out of
Baker Street on the corner by Selfridge's, Lucy senses a presence around her. From where she sits at the front of the top of
the bus, she watches as Oxford Street stretches a mile straight
ahead: she watches as Oxford Street turns in that light from
that height at that moment into a shimmering Paris, into a
boulevard aimed through a canvas, into a sight signed *Pissarro*:

'Hello, Lucie.'

'Oh, hello, Camille.'

'May I sit?'

'But of course. I was just thinking about you.'

(He sits beside her. They are speaking in French:)

'I, myself,' he admits, 'have been thinking all morning.
About coloured rain.'

(He totes a Selfridge's bag, which he holds on his knees. His
legs are long and abut on the upper deck window. The veins in
his hands are like grapevines in winter:)

'But you've been shopping, Camille,' Lucy takes note.

(He sighs, in replying:) 'I purchased a hat. Would you see it?'

'I would, very much.'

'Then for you, my dear Lucie: I'll don it.'

(He draws from the bag a deerstalker cap; puts it on. Its
earflaps are tied at the crown with brown ribbon.)

'What do you think?' he asks (striking a pose: His beard
billows over his chest; his artist's smock's splattered with burn
holes and ochre).

'Oh, really, Camille: it's *you*,' Lucy answers.

'Not too English?'

'Oh, no, Camille. You carry it off.'

'It's the nose,' he admits. 'I own a nose made for hats. But
where are you going, dear Lucie?'

'Why, to the Gallery, Camille. Same as always.'

'Same as I! We will travel together! I'm meeting Degas there today!'

'What, *Edgar*? I thought you weren't speaking.'

'Who tells you such lies?!'

'Well, I . . .'

'What flat-hearted, forked-penis, poor-as-a-begger, blind bastard is spreading such lies?! But of course we have had, what you say, fallings out! We are always not speaking! We have temperament! We are hot-blooded men! We have the blood in our eyes! What is a *moment*, I ask you, except such a thing that is fixed to be *un*-fixed? I, Pissarro, not speaking to Degas? We painted *light*, can you not understand? We painted Light! What is the Universe? What are the stars? Aren't they Light? Take this hat! What is this hat? Can you eat it? We were starving! We were selling our souls to the devil for pigments! I wore these hats to remember to beg – I wore these hats to pass them around! Yes, we had terrible arguments! There were days, weeks and months when we each of us weren't on this earth, when we acted like gods – Degas wouldn't speak with Cassatt – Cézanne wouldn't go to see Zola – Claude fought with Edouard over *black* – Gauguin fought with Seurat over *scale* of a canvas – everyone argued with everyone else, because each one believed she or he owned the deed to the landscape of Heaven, except *me*: Monsieur Pissarro. I argued with no one. Never. Not once. Not even for Dreyfus – I was the one who made peace. I was the 'Old Man'. The 'Ancient'. Pissarro. I couldn't believe human nature is venal. I had to believe human nature is good, to keep painting. Without painting . . .' (He gestures:) 'All *this* would be lost. But you understand. You've been in love I am sure . . .'

'Many times.'

'Ah, yes, same as I. Many times. Many times. With the same woman. You are meeting your lover today?'

'Most likely, Camille.'

'You have a date?'

'Not exactly.'

'A rendez-vous?'

'He shows up, different times. He appears.'

'Why are you telling me lies?! A woman like you must be loved and adored with devotion and valour!'

'Camille, calm yourself. One mustn't rant on a bus, here in London.'

'You are too lovely! Too charming! Too lively a woman not to be loved and adored!'

'Yes, I know, Camille: (but people are *staring* at us!)'

'Let them stare! We are landscapes! We're our own works of art!'

'(But not *in public*, Camille!)'

'Not "in public", but where, then? *Where*, then?' (He stands up, making a speech to the passengers:) 'Where should a man be *a man*? In his dress? In his mind? In his manners? But, no! In his passion! We are not *bees* in a *hive* making *honey*! We are *men* in a *life* making –'

'This is our stop,' Lucy tells him. 'Let's go.'

They depart. As they do, they are met by Degas:

'Stay as you are! Stop like that! Guard this moment!' (He sets up his camera.)

'*Merde*,' Camille swears: 'He'll keep us like this, fixed here, forever . . .'

(Degas plays with his tripod, shouting his orders, *That's it! Hold the air in your lungs!*) Camille whispers to Lucy, 'See him? The world's foremost draftsman, looking at us through a keyhole!' (After a minute, Degas cries, *It's ruined! A cloud's on the sun! We'll start over!*) 'Never,' Camille says: 'Lucie must go. She's meeting her lover.'

'*What* lover?' Degas demands. 'What are you saying?! There's Love and there's Art and we have but one *heart*: We'll start over.'

'She's leaving,' he's told.

'Women!' he shouts. (He packs up his tripod.) 'All they think

about is lemonade! Sometimes, on good days, they think about
. . . *Switzerland!*'

'All *you* ever think of are *buttocks!*' Pissarro shouts back.

Edgar yells: 'And all *you* think of are Jews! Jews and *peasants!*'

'Jews and peasants, oh, *yes!* But never their *buttocks* –!'

'A man who makes *crossroads* a theme!' Degas shouts.

'A man who spies women through *keyholes!*'

'My brother!'

'My friend!'

(They leave together:) Lucy sighs. *Why are men so difficult?* she
wonders. She mounts the stairs to the National Gallery and
pauses, under the portico, to watch the sky expand over the
square. From somewhere two bright balloons, one red and one
yellow, belonging to children, float, lost in the sky. Mary
Cassatt stops beside her:

'Hello, Lucy.'

(Miss Cassatt rests her hands on the stone balustrade and
takes in the view sweeping down Whitehall toward Parliament.
She's an elegant, practical woman. When she speaks, she
sounds just like Kate Hepburn:)

'Watch out for Edgar,' she says. 'He's armed with his camera
today.'

'I know – I saw him.'

'He's not around here, I hope?'

'He went off with Camille.'

'Which direction?'

'*That* way.'

'Good, then: I'll go in the other.' (She unfurls her parasol and
straightens her shoulders. Being a lady, she asks,) 'Are you
meeting your lover today?'

'Yes, I am.'

'Well, that's good. I hope he's not nasty like Edgar.'

'Edgar's not nasty.'

'Edgar *Degas?* Isn't nasty? He certainly *is.*'

'No, he's not.'

'He doesn't like people of *our sex*, my dear. He doesn't like our
sex at all.'

'He *paints* like he does.'

'What does that prove? Painting's not absolute. The eye is
subjective. Sometimes the eye is a rose-coloured lens. What
would it seem that *I* like, then – judging my painting?'

'Oh, babies.'

'Not women?'

'Women in hats.'

'Not *men*?'

'Men with babies.'

'Well, there you are.'

(She disappears.)

The problem with so many geniuses, Lucy decides, *is that they rarely
makes sense when they talk.*

She steps from the sunlight into the National Gallery and
feels a welcome security almost at once, as if she were newly
back home. She likes the smell of the place, an aroma combin-
ing damp stucco, worn carpets and wormwood. She likes the
moment of choice one must take in the foyer to turn to the left or
the right at the top of the stairs. She has a contract of faith to
turn to the right, toward the XXth Century, but often she
pauses, as all lovers must, only to wonder what light might
exist, outside commitment, elsewhere.

As she walks up the stairs to the right, past a palm tree, her
heartbeat increases. Through these doors, she well knows,
waits a moment, a stranger, a lover, the future, unknown. Time
and the ribbon of materiality will ravel themselves through the
space of a canvas and once more, she knows, she will enter new
worlds. Each time she travels within she discovers her senses
anew; she grows younger, her skin takes on hues of transcen-
dence, her face and hair give off radiance, she balances
somewhere, a place that seems lighter than Light:

'Hello, Lucie.'

'Oh, Monsieur Monet! You gave me a fright!'

'Me, too. I'm sorry. I frighten myself, when I speak. One shouldn't speak. It ruins the silence. It ripples the water. It ruffles the air. It wakes up the fishes.'

'But think of a world where people don't speak,' Lucy tells him, 'how sad it would be.'

(He stares at her, blankly:) 'Sad?' he repeats.

'Yes, and lonely.'

'Well, which?'

'Sad and lonely – they're one and the same.'

'Oh but sad moves. The emotion of sadness has movement. Lonely . . . that's stillness. A stillness without and within. Have you never been lonely?'

'Who, me? Oh not me, Monsieur. Oh no. Never. I'm never lonely. I've never been lonely. Not for an instant. What I meant is, it *would* be sad. To be lonely. Not speaking. Bound in a silence as if by a frame, like these pictures . . .'

'You find these pictures sad, then, do you, Lucie?'

'Sometimes. Yes. I do.'

'But beautiful, nevertheless?'

'Always beautiful.'

'So do I. Especially *mine*.'

(He wanders off) and leaves Lucy standing in Room 44. On one side, there are several Pissarros, a Degas, two Daumiers, a corner of Corots, a Corbet, a Delacroix and two smooth placid Ingres, glowing like eggs in aspic. Then, on the opposite side of the room, there are nothing but Imps. Thirteen of them, gathered like stars in formation, winking their promise of worlds in the distance: *The Thames Below Westminster, The Beach at Trouville, Music in the Tuileries Gardens, The Gare St. Lazare, The Seine at Asnières, Bathers at Grenouillère* . . .

'Oh in those days the world could still laugh,' Renoir is saying.

'*Pah!*' he is answered, after a beat, by Cézanne.

(They have set up their travelling easels, Cézanne in front of Renoir so he can't watch the other's swift progress with colour.

Today, Renoir is painting a copy of Monet's *The Beach at Trouville*, and Cézanne is trying to work out a copy of Degas's *Young Spartans*:)

'What talent! What talent!' Renoir remarks, failing to specify whose.

'Shut up, you cow,' Cézanne growls.

'You see, Lucie,' Renoir instructs, 'how Monet laid down the lead white here with the smallest of quantities of pure prussian blue, and a dab of his own cobalt violet. Look at the sand. There is sand in the painting. Stand closer, see it? Grains of real sand! Isn't that marvelous? Painting *en plein air*! Open-air painting! Those were the days, weren't they, Paul?'

'May a pigeon fly over and shit on your canvas,' Cézanne commands.

'Then the critics would think it was yours – Aren't you finished yet?'

(Cézanne stares at his canvas:)

'I've laid down eight strokes.'

'Eight brushstrokes?'

'One less than nine.'

'For three hours' work?'

'*With so much noise, am I also expected to* paint?'

'May I see what you've done?' Lucy asks him.

'*Are you out of your mind?!*'

(He puts his fist through the canvas. Renoir hurries him out, before he can start to destroy every painting of his in the Gallery. They leave Lucy) to stand by herself near the south wall in front of Manet's *The Execution of Maximilian*. Two figures enter behind her. She turns to regard them. Through opposite doors there have entered a young man who's handsomely dressed, darkly foreign; and a young woman, too tongue-tied to speak. They move 'round the room with the balance of proton to neutron, creating a silence between them which quavers. The young woman is faintly aware of the young man circling elsewhere in the room as she stops to regard a Monet with deliberate attention. There's *sand* in the picture, she notes, grains of real sand. As she senses the young man approaching behind her, she strolls to the opposite side of the room. She's wearing a brown-coloured travelling suit, very prim, very proper, over an ivory silk camisole; and a choker of triple-strand pearls. She's clutching a guidebook and holding her gloves in her hand. Except for her nervousness one might expect from the way she was dressed that she was a woman of thirty-or-so, but she was much younger than that when this happened. Lucy is stunned at how young she looked then. The young man is a traveller, too, she can tell by the way that he's dressed; and he's wearing cologne which is not at all masculine, that is to say, not at all like the scent of her father's.

'What a strange painting,' he suddenly says, standing beside her in front of the Degas.

The young woman turns her face toward him a moment too soon for their eyes not to meet. His are deep brown with thick eyelashes like brushes. She blushes. She feels herself tingle. She senses the young man along her full length. She feels him come ever so slightly a little bit nearer to her. She feels the cool air of his breath on her neck by her ear. She is keenly aware he might touch her. Then her eyes see a breast, not a painting, a nipple, a breast, not a line, not a brushstroke, a nipple, a breast, a boy's penis, a buttocks, bare flesh and bare-breasted girls like herself and their nipples. The other boy's penis. She parts her lips.

'I wonder, if I might be so bold,' the young man begins.

'You may not,' she can barely reply.

She turns and walks briskly away, her hands clutching her gloves and the guidebook, her head held in a way that speaks of her pride in having escaped a lapse of decorum, her posture complete in its self-satisfaction, not worn down, Lucy notes, as it will be these fifty years later, by haunting regrets. You are a dotty old woman, she says to herself. Well, perhaps, but so what? she agrees. Less dotty now than I was way back then. Carlo was just going to ask me to visit his villa in Naples. Of course I accepted. A week proved a lifetime. Of couse we knew *everyone* then. I sat for Matisse by the Bay. Even the births of our seven children couldn't detract from my *bella figura*. And Carlo, of course, never aged. Always handsome. *Adoro.* A wonderful dancer. The kindest of men. The gentlest of lovers, knowing I came from a convent. A hero. In war? Not war. I wouldn't have let him. A martyr. A pacifist. He joined the Resistance. I did, too. Was he killed? He was wounded. We were wounded together. He had to walk with a cane. Maybe not. There was the thing with the dancing. He lost a finger, that's all. Could I stand being touched by a man with four fingers? He had a *scar*. Yes. That's better. He had a *scar* from a *Befehlshaber*'s saber . . .

Outside the museum the sun is just setting and Manet appears.

'Hello, Lucie.'

'Oh, hello, Edouard.'

She begins to descend the broad stairs, toward the square.

'I wonder, if I may be so bold,' Edouard requests, 'may I ask to walk with you?'

'Sure,' Lucy says. 'Please yourself.'

(He links her arm through his own and leads them to stroll 'round the fountains in gorgeous rose-coloured light.)

'Did you meet your lover this afternoon?' he asks, politely.

'Oh yes.'

'Is he very handsome?'

'Yes, he is.'

'Have you known him for long?'

'Since we were young.'

'Tell me. What does he say?'

'He comes toward me and stands very close.'

'But does he speak?'

'We look at each other. We stare and we stare until the edges of the things around us start to grow invisible.'

'But does he never speak?'

'Until the world itself begins to grow invisible, until the only thing we see is what exists between two lovers.'

(Manet stares into the sun.)

'Ah yes,' he says. 'Ah yes. Ah yes. Ah yes. I've seen it.'

Herself in Love

Here's what women say, they say: 'I loved him for his way with words, I loved the skin around his eyes.' They sub-divide their men, they apportion to them grassy knolls on which to lollygag, they create swamp bogs (the things they cannot love) and bottomlands (the areas with margins for improvements). They make mental lists: his nails, his teeth, his nose hairs. They think of men not so much as objects of their love but as a project that comes wrapped at Christmas, disassembled. His gentleness with dishes. His 'visions'. His wretched socks. The way he tells a joke, the way he shifts the Datsun. The way he lifts his head from kisses on our breasts and gives us back a breath of our perfume. His naïveté in face of doom. His stomach muscles and the sweep of his long back.

A man is something which is nothing like the full sum of its parts – the way a snow crystal is not. A little dust, a little air, a little water at high altitude do not freeze the mind in wondrous contemplation of the universe until, in combination, catching on a random tuft of crimson scarf, a snowflake, fluidizing, breaks a woman's heart.

What women say, they say: 'He hit me like a ton of bricks. He took my breath away. He unhinged me and I started shaking. He undid me. He has done me in.' They turn tin ears on the music of the spheres and talk about his *skin* his *smile* his *tender failings*. No enigma equals the obscurity of how a woman tries to justify her love. Love is not a theft; or is it. Love is not a treason, is it. Love is not a perjury, or crime. It cannot kill, or can it. It will not test the morals of a race, or raze civilization. It won't annihilate the native vegetation. It may not even exist. As God might not. Why bother with it.

But women say, they say: 'I can't go on without him. I think about him night and day. He turns me inside-out.' They say, 'He has *spaces* between his fingers. He has *fine hairs* along his shoulders. He has *toes*.' It's as though discovery of the other sex, the sense of parts apart, discloses brand new meaning on existence. 'I never knew who *I* was *'til*,' they say, he kissed me or he touched me or he closed his eyes and laid his head down and said 'thank you'.

Herself had had that kind of bliss and 'You can keep it' was her attitude. Herself had said 'No more.' No more love for her. No more staring pie-eyed at the farthest wall, no more starving, no more feasting, no more fast breaks from routine. The work at hand was far too arduous *a menos de amor*. The work at hand was Living:

In walked Killebrew.

Killebrew that bastard couldn't put two things together without causing one of them to break out in a rash. Herself was decent, ordered, sedulous, just. Killebrew was seepage. 'Oh god, it's Killebrew,' herself might say in much the same way as, 'Oh god, the sink is leaking.' Killebrew appeared from time to time like water on the floor inside a house. Unwanted news.

172

You'd think if love were going to strike there'd be a sign, some *frissonnement*, the birds gone suddenly, scaremongeringly, *mute*. But nothing outside the mere ordinary graced the day, a Thursday, garbage pick-up day, when Killebrew accumulated like a puddle on her side of the road.

'Hey, Killebrew,' she acknowledged.

'How's herself?' he said.

'Not bad. How's yours?'

'The same. I've been ringing your credenza there for half an hour.'

He pointed toward the door. *Credenza* in this case might signify her doorbell. Or it might not. With Killebrew one never knew.

'So what's up?' she asked, while surveying him: motely moldy workpants with perhaps no zipper in the fly; workboots; several tattered layers of several tattered shirts topped with a red hooded sweatshirt bunched and tied around his face so he resembled Rumpelstiltskin in a baby bunting.

'Use your phone,' he said.

'Sure. Wander in, you'll find it.' She started walking up the driveway toward the backyard garbage bin. He fell in beside her. 'What are you up to this morning?' he asked. He seemed to have forgotten his request to use her phone. 'You like my sweatshirt?' he asked. He pulled two little peaks of it out from his topography and read the chest logo out loud as though he'd just discovered it: ' "NOAA". Know what that stands for?'

'Nope.'

'Me neither,' he admitted.

'National Organization of Another Annoyance?' she guessed.

'Yep, that's me.'

'I guess you'll want a cup of coffee, too,' she guessed again.

'Oh, no, just the check will do, thank you . . .'

Inside her house he wandered through the downstairs 'til he found the phone. It was an old house and the phone had been

installed in a small front room by some windows. When herself
moved in she'd left the phone where she had found it. It seemed
inordinately housewifely to have a phone moved to the kitchen.
As though a caller might expect to find her there. Battering
fried chicken.

'Fred?' she heard him say. 'Is Fred there? Fred is *out*? Well
when's he due? No. Fine. No problem. I'll call back.'

Killebrew came back into the kitchen, took his sweatshirt off,
and sat down on the blue stool by the stove. Then he stood up,
took a coffee cup from her cabinet and poured himself a cup of
coffee. 'Murphy's out, the dumb mullah,' he announced.
'Lucky thing I didn't go up there on time.' Then he sat
down.

'You want milk?' she asked.

He shook his head.

She leaned against the dishwasher and stared at him and
thought this would be as good a time as any to start baking the
rum raisin cake for Christmas. 'Mind if I go about my chores?'
she said.

'No, go right ahead. You like my sweater?'

There had been a sweater underneath the sweatshirt.

'It's very nice,' she said.

He made the same gesture he had made before, lifting out the
fabric with his thumb and forefinger.

'Did you get it at the thrift shop?' she asked, conversationally.

'It's brand new!' he protested. 'Cosmic knitted it, my birth-
day was last week.'

' "Cosmic"?'

'And she never knitted anything before.'

'Well, it's very nice. It will keep you very warm.' It looked
like vacuum cleaner fuzz, she thought. 'Who's "Cosmic"?' And
because she didn't really care, she read the recipe: ' "Put the
raisins in a bowl and add the rum. Let stand overnight. Stir
occasionally." Now *that's* real comic writing . . .'

'You don't know about The Cosmic and myself? Been going

on about four months. Call her The Cosmic Korean. After my divorce I took the pledge, you know: no more white women.'

He looked at her.

'Yeah, they say whole wheat's a whole lot better for you,' she said, pointedly.

'Definitely. Or rye,' he answered. She heard it 'wry'.

He got up, left the kitchen, made another phone call and came back.

'One third cup dark rum to one cup raisins seems like a lot of rum to me,' she said. She measured out the rum and poured it on the raisins. She looked worried. Killebrew came over and peered inside the bowl. 'Those babies will sop it up in no time,' he maintained. He lifted the rum bottle by its neck and took a large swallow of it. He lit a cigarette. He walked into the pantry, stared at all her plates and came back into the kitchen with an ashtray. He sat down.

'"Sift together" . . . Right, I did that. "A quarter teaspoon salt," it says: "*if desired*" . . .'

'Don't use it,' he said, emphatically.

She looked at him. 'No?'

'No salt.'

'Sometimes salt, though, brings out sweetness. Heightens it . . .'

He was staring at her. He stood up, walked to the sink, put his cigarette out with running water and lit another. He left the room to make another call. She heard him say, 'Fred? Killebrew. I'm socked in here in town so I'll be running late. A little late. How late? It won't be *days*, all right?' She thought, This is ridiculous – I don't want to bake this *cake*. I want him to *leave*. He came back into the kitchen and she thought, Ten minutes more and then you're finished, Killebrew.

They talked about a movie they had both just seen. They talked about a book or two, while he poured himself another cup of coffee and smoked another cigarette. She set aside the

dry ingredients, chopped the walnuts, watched the clock.
'"Freshly grated nutmeg",' she read: 'Give me a break.' She
crossed the kitchen to the spice cabinet. 'That's the sort of
instruction we ignore, right? Like "Whip to strong peaks over
ice" –' She turned to smile at him and he was leaning at the
counter, bent a little, both hands on his heart.

'John, what the hell –?'

He stared at her.

'For godsake, are you all right?'

'No. What? I'm with you.'

He began to pace.

'Are you having an attack?'

'What? No.'

'Are you in pain?'

'Pain? No. Yes. I don't know. My heart was beating very
fast.'

'Are you having palpitations?'

'No.'

'Sit down.'

'No. Fine. I'm fine. It's going to pass.'

'For godsake, it's the coffee. I put in these espresso beans, not
everyone can –'

'Not the coffee.'

'Plus two cigarettes.'

'Not the cigarettes.'

'And rum.'

'Oh, lady, lots of rum.'

'Anxiety attack. Or stress. You're late for that appoint-
ment . . .'

'No.'

'Do you have to do something today that you don't want to
do? That could be the cause of the anxiety.'

'I don't have to do a single thing today that I don't want to
do. In fact, I don't have to do a thing, if I don't want to.'

'Well, then, Killebrew, it's cigarettes.'

She turned back to the recipe and its freshly grated rinds of
lemons.

'In fact,' he said, 'it is anxiety.'

He came to stand quite near her, then moved away.

'It *is* anxiety. It's anxiety over not being able to know how to
start to begin to say what I'm going to say.'

She smiled at him, as an encouragement, and walked over to
the refrigerator and took out two lemons. He stopped. She
looked at him. 'Do I have to be over there,' she joked, pointing
to where he stood, 'for you to say it?'

'Yes, m'am.'

She returned.

With the lemons.

He sat down at the table a foot or so from where she was
working. The scene smelled of rum, the open jar of nutmeg,
and, now as she was grating it, tart lemon. 'I wanted to say,
what I didn't know if I was going to be able to say was how
really nice it is, it's really nice, to come around and sit and drink
your coffee and just talk to you . . .'

She looked up and smiled and tilted her head and said, 'Why,
thank you, Killebrew.'

'. . . And then the other thing, when I was sitting over there,'
– he pointed to the blue stool by the stove; she grated – 'I was
sitting over there and I was thinking why am I sitting here when
I really want to walk over there' – he pointed to where she was
standing – 'and just kiss your face.'

For what seemed a long time she stared at the lemon in her
left hand and its odd grater in the other. Then she laid the
lemon and the grater down. It seemed to her that some response
was necessary and it seemed to her that anything that she could
say would be an insult to his sensibility and that the only thing
that she could do with any rightness would be bend to him and
give him a sweet kiss right on his cheek and when she did that he
very gently turned her lips to his and they were kissing. Soon,
somehow, they were standing, too, and kissing and the aroma of

the lemon from her hands encompassed them. 'I want you,' he whispered. 'I've always wanted to make love to you. I've always acted like a gentleman.'

'We would make very tenderhearted love,' she heard herself observe.

After a while he murmured, 'Let's go upstairs.' She held her breath and considered the idea. 'Oh, no,' he said. 'Oh, no, don't frown.' He placed his lips between her eyebrows where years had traced a worry line. 'I'll leave, if that's what you think I should do,' he suggested, but he didn't budge. She heard herself admit, 'If we don't do it now, we'll never do it.'

'Then let's do it.'

She sighed. 'Well, alright, John.'

He started to lead her to the stairs. 'You sound so enthusiastic about it. You'll see. This is a great idea.'

'It's not a *great* idea, John,' she said, climbing the stairs in front of him.

'You'll see. It's a good idea.'

'It's not the best idea I've ever heard . . .'

'Oh, no, you're right. Print this on the front page of the *Times* and people won't say *that's* the best idea I've ever heard, but you'll see. It's a good idea . . .'

Better than most.

In a little while, he was getting dressed again. 'Are you leaving?' she asked. It was a stupid question.

He sat down on the bed next to where she lay and tied his shoes. 'I wasn't even thinking about this when I woke up this morning,' he explained. 'You weren't even on my mind – I guess you were. Yeah, I think you were. I think I thought about you late last night. I was writing a letter to this girl named Connie that I knew once in the third grade back in Buffalo and I was trying to explain my life and this letter just kept going on and going on and I thought, Jesus, who could I ever show this to and I thought of you. I wasn't even writing it to Connie, after a while. I don't know *who* I was writing it to. To whom.' He took her hand. 'Then, I swear to God, I just stopped by your house to use your phone and my heart started pounding. I've never had that happen. Once. One time before. And I thought, John, boy, you've got to say something to her, or you've got to get your coat on and get out the door.'

'You weren't wearing a coat, John.'

'It's allegorical.' He kissed her. 'See me out?'

'No.'

'*No?*'

'I'm staying in bed.' She pulled a pillow close to her. 'I'm somewhere close to being in a dream state . . .'

'Well, you're right there. That says it.' He looked at her and said, 'This whole thing's put me on "Stun" . . .'

Friday she didn't run into him in town; nor Saturday. On Sunday she ran into him on Main Street when she went to buy her Sunday papers. He was with a group of other men, dressed for heavy weather, autumn water; scallopers. He looked guilty of contrition and a mite confused. 'Hey, Killebrew,' she acknowledged. 'How's herself?' he asked. The other men were watching carefully to see if something dropped. 'I'm well,' she nodded. 'And how's *your* health, John?' His eyes revealed a clear understanding of her frame of reference, and a tinge of panic that accompanies the proximity to an incendiary substance. She slipped her hand inside her coat and laid her palm across one breast so everyone could see and said, 'No more heart palpitations?'

'No, m'am,' he said, smiling, walking backwards. 'Got that matter well in hand. I saw a specialist.'

'Well, good. You must be real glad it didn't keep you on my back for long –'

She colored furiously.

She'd meant to say, *your* back.

*

Monday came and went and Tuesday morning around ten o'clock she was unloading from her car some kindling she had gathered when Killebrew pulled up. He sat staring at her from the cab of his truck until she walked over to him. 'Hey, Killebrew,' she said. She thought she ought to be real angry with him but instead she started noticing the skin around his eyes, the different colors intermingling in his beard. 'This is for you,' he said. He handed her a file folder with a few typed pages in it. 'It's the letter I started writing to that girl I used to know in the third grade back in Buffalo. Connie. She and I and her kid brother and my brother Rick grew up together. Long time ago.' He touched a piece of tree bark where it had caught in the loose weave on the cuff of her sweater. 'You shouldn't stand out in the rain,' he told her. She hadn't even noticed it was raining. She said, 'Can I give you a cup of coffee?' He held up a chipped mug of coffee and said, 'I have mine,' but he got out of the truck anyway. They walked up the front porch steps and he said, 'Is it after ten o'clock? I promised this old geezer on Hines Point I'd drop off my sander by ten o'clock. He's got the whole day planned around my sander . . .'

They were in the kitchen and she had taken down a clean cup from the cabinet for herself and gone to the refrigerator for the quart of milk and instead of letting the refrigerator door close automatically, she slammed it. They stared at one another. 'Can I kiss you?' she asked. That part of her that's always squaring edges, crossing out, correcting, justifying, thought 'Can'? *Can* I kiss you? Almost imperceptibly he nodded, yes. In less than a minute they were starting up the stairs, Killebrew shedding his sweater as he went and four minutes later he was lacing up his boots on his way down.

She thought her clock had stopped.

'What are we calling this, "The Phantom Strikes"?' she asked.

'I'm really sorry. No kidding. I wasn't going to come here.

Swear to God. This geezer on Hines Point is such a nice old
guy . . .'

John was leaving, half undressed.

She, herself, was in her bare feet, t-shirt and her underwear.
He had gotten up as if the house had been on fire and she had
followed right along with him.

'If you can find some time to read my letter I'll appreciate it.
It won't take you long to read. It won't take up too much of your
time.'

'John, nothing could take less time than this –'

He put his arms around her and held her securely and kissed
her. 'Thank you,' he told her.

'For godsake, Killebrew, you don't say "thank you" to a
lover.'

'Right. You're right there. I'll go home and look that up in
Webster's and it'll say "Not said to a lover" . . .'

The letter started workmanlike enough: Dear Connie, comma.
He'd moved away, he'd gotten married, he'd dodged the draft,
he'd had a son. He'd lived in Arizona where his marriage fell
apart. He'd worked his trade and made a living, moved around;
then finally followed his estranged wife and their son back East
to this small fishing village on the bay. That seemed to sum it
up, he wrote, except that that suggested a black vacuum at the
center of his life into which his past, his present and his future
seemed to float. And maybe that was why he was sitting down
to try to write these things. To try to find out where the
emptiness came from. Why it existed. When it had begun. Most
people didn't understand what he did for a living, he wrote. Or
what it meant to him. He was a carpenter. A good one. Most
people thought of that profession as being 'in the trades'. And it
was true, sometimes to pay his way he had to take the nothing
job, nail-banging job. But what he loved to do was finework.
Beading a moulding with a nineteenth century Stanley #45

Jack plane. Working wood: wood working. 'I've seen men sign the top tread of a gooseneck staircase before fastening it in place,' he wrote. 'I've seen descriptions of the weather of the day on the back of mouldings applied sixty-five years ago, as well as a sequential signing of men who have removed the same moulding. Five names in sixty-five years. Names of extinct millhouses, newspapers – a crew of mine wrote a fifty chapter novel describing the exploits of, the building of, a house on its framing, to be covered for years to come by wallboard. I personally have taken to putting Latin epigrams and the latest barometric pressure on the back or bottom of piecework as an encouragement to those anonymous artisans, for whom the work is always more important than their names. I admire the ability of those,' the letter ended, 'who could spend fifteen or twenty years building a cathedral. I guess I'm sorry that I'll never get that chance.'

She thought, Love is a Revelation, like a religion, some religions; like Islam. She thought about the tile-cutters, the tile-layers, the mosaicists of mosques. She thought about cathedral spires and pagodas. She thought about the artist's handprint on the cavewall at Lascaux. She thought about what sets humans apart – their art, their fossilizing edifices, love, and their devotion to their sense of time. But time is bogus. Time does not exist in any universal way. It's not the thread that twines through heaven – like gravity, the condition time imposes is exact, but not eternal. The act of even thinking of eternity is a captive act of sitting in time's trap. Without time, what is there. Days of staring pie-eyed at the farthest wall. Minutes leaning on a rake. Hours lost in random conversation.
Nights on 'Stun'.
'It's after one.'
'It isn't.'
'Yes.'

'It can't be.'

'Right you are. You're right there. In Vladivostok, it's not one. But around here, vampires are thinking about lunch . . .'

They had been talking for five hours – making love, and talking. The candles had burned down on her bedside tables and her bedroom seemed a berth inside a floating ship. They had talked about their families and their pasts. Or, *he* had talked and she had listened. It seemed a natural balance, effortless, the way he talked; she listened. His way with words. They'd been lovers ten days, not that she was counting. A week from now, a month, a year: what then. Maybe they would dish their manic clever selves off cliffs into black water.

Here's what women think, they think: Forever.

'Tell me about Connie,' she said.

'Connie. *Consuelo*,' he breathed. He settled down against the pillow and wrapped her in his arms. 'She and I and her kid brother and my brother Rick were trouble on a stick in the third grade. Wasn't anything that could hold still between us. We were thick as thieves. Called ourselves the Chicken Eaters. I was Chicken John. Rick was Chicken Rick. Joe was Chicken Joe. And Con was Chicken Con. Then one day we were running chicken drills down by the river. We were standing in this burned out rubble field by the Niagara and we all, together, got to feeling really weird. Chicken Con, she was a real tomboy and I never saw her do a single thing that anyone could classify as sissy, but she took hold of my hand. They were diverting the water from the American Fall so they could measure its erosion. Whole bunch of geodesic gnomes from the Army Corps of Engineers. Big program. And us kids were standing down there by the river and this wall of water starts coming through the plain, this enormous wall, water backed up all over itself and the *sound* it makes is just amazing, it must have been, well, I don't know because we were all just kids, it must have been three or four storeys high. And Chicken Con, she got this mean determined look on not to be too scared and she takes hold of

183

my hand. Then, the next thing that you know, it's come and
gone. It was all over in a minute. There was nothing we could
do but stand right there and stare at it. The most amazing
thing. So that's who Connie is.'

She wanted to say, 'I love you, John.'

She lay against him, as if she were his shore and she wanted
to say, 'I love you, John,' but something told her he would turn
to her and tell her 'thank you' so she lay there, watching him,
for what may have passed as hours as he turned in sleep and
rolled, inexorably, toward dreaming.